THE TRAVELER: BECOMING POWER

THE TRAVELER
BOOK THREE

DEBORAH DUGAN

To my family, for being awesome.

ACKNOWLEDGMENTS

Thank you,

All my beta readers group members for providing your invaluable insights.

Miss Jessica for vetting ideas that seemed unworkable.

Nurse Julie for confirming ER release procedures.

WIKIPEDIA!!

INTRODUCTION

I spend a lot of thinking time in the "what if" zone. What would happen if a being was functionally immortal, but was only intermittently engaged with the physical world? How would that being develop, and what would it look like? What would need to change in order for that being to survive? When writing a book, each of those questions requires a plausible resolution within the context of the story. There are permutations within each such resolution, expanding outward like ripples from a stone thrown into still water, which take the author into the "if/then" zone. It is definitely possible to write oneself into a corner, and it can take some time to get extricated and move on to the next question. I had a fabulous time writing The Traveler. I stretched into unknown areas and made connections that were surprising. It was fascinating, knowing that I didn't know what Harry was going to get up to when I sat down in front of my computer. I couldn't wait to find out! Harry has a long future ahead of him, and I hope you'll join him on his continuing travels.

FOREWORD

This book can be read as a standalone novel, but reading the series in order will provide a much more satisfactory understanding of the Traveler's origin and history so far.

This is the third book in the series where we follow the Traveler's adventures through time, which is not at all to say the Traveler moves through time in the "normal" fashion of time travel. The Traveler is functionally immortal; he has lived thousands of lives but, instead of dying at the end of each life, he is reborn. He has never left his planet of origin, yet he is utterly alien to humans. The story of the Traveler and his time-bound companions is one of multiple First Contacts that have occurred throughout human history.

When Harry introduced himself to Tristan, it proved to be a rocky start to their ultimately deep friendship. After recovering from his initial disbelief and intense shock upon first seeing Harry, Tristan was convinced Harry was a robot, and that Tristan's friend, Dan, was the instigator of an intricate, somewhat malicious, prank. Tristan assumed Dan was somehow remotely seeing and hearing through Harry. After recovering from his initial trauma, Tristan had questions, but Harry's answers weren't completely illuminating:

> "I have to say I have questions for you, Dan, so many questions. Just to start with, how in the hell did you get it into my bathroom vent? I never heard a thing until it was moving around in there. How is this robot communicating with me? I've seen lots of different types of robots on television and in movies, but this one is really something. I certainly have never interacted with a robot like this."

> *"Uh, Dan's not here, man. Are you sure you're okay? Am I ever glad you settled down for a chat, though. Usually I just get one word out and all of a sudden there are boots flying, people screaming, flamethrowers, whatever. I actually saw someone with a pitchfork once, true story. People just don't get me, know what I mean? Dude, this one time—well, never mind that."*

Tristan was extremely reluctant to accept that Harry was in fact a living, intelligent, non-human being—one who could "talk" using what Harry termed "universal vibrations." Harry hadn't always been able to talk in such a manner. It was something he'd had to learn, in another relatively recent lifetime. Unfortunately, due to the vagaries of his existence, Harry's memories of his past lives were fragmentary. He couldn't remember how he had come to understand the theory of universal vibrations, much less quantum mechanics and particle physics. In his current lifetime, after much effort, Harry was able to convince Tristan that Harry is not a robot. In the end, the two came to highly value each other's companionship, and Harry was able to share with Tristan a glimpse of one of Harry's past lives. It is only one of the adventures Harry will come to share with his human friends.

Harry's transformation to his current physical configuration began when the planet's surface was itself being transformed. A chance lightning strike, momentarily holding a microcosm of the sun's incandescent power, energized a single cell floating in a tidal pool, causing that single cell to begin the process of becoming a multicellular mite. After a time, lightning found the tidal pool again; this time the energy caused the beginning formation of a nascent brain. Eventually, the mite had been reconfigured into a proto-animal, which became caught in a tidal surge that washed it into the ocean. Violent storm winds and towering ocean waves created a whirlpool into which the proto-animal was dragged, its tentacles flailing behind it as it was spun, held against the wall of the rapidly spinning whirlpool. Lightning found it again, striking the water directly above the proto-animal as it spun. The whirlpool gathered the energy of the lightning strike, and the proto-animal was enveloped in energy as it spun.

The energy that enfolded the proto-animal did not fade

completely; some remnant remained captured in its cells. The forces exerted by the spinning whirlpool, together with the captured lightning energy, combined to create a chemical process unique in the universe, and unique to this proto-animal only. The proto-animal felt an urge to drive itself to the darker, deeper reaches of the ocean, and then another that drove it to dig a long, sloping tunnel into the ocean bed. Curled into a small space at the end of the tunnel, the proto- animal's new chemical processes put it into stasis, a state in which it would remain for millennia after millennia. As it slept, the proto-animal would continue to change, to evolve from within its own form. Eventually, the proto-animal 's epoch-spanning journey from the ocean depths to dry land resulted in a being of seemingly unlimited hunger and no intelligence, other than the instinct to feed.

Many ages later, after unknown numbers of stasis periods, the being had evolved into a four-limbed creature that lived in the forests of the land in which it had last awoken. That version of the being still had no awareness of self, and its primary goal was to avoid becoming prey. Many millennia later yet, the being awoke again to find it had evolved into a humanoid body, with a fierce intelligence and special abilities to manage internal and external energy flows. Sentience, and finally self-knowledge, had developed in tandem with physical changes.

After untold millions of years, through innumerable geologic ages, the being that began as the proto-animal alter-nately lived its lives and slept through periods of stasis, during which its physical transformation continued to evolve, until it became Harry's present-day configuration. All his lives remained connected through time by a thread of seeming immortality. His many names have hung from that thread, each name ephemeral within the evanescent ebb and flow of

Harry's lives. He had lived many thousands of lives with no name and wasn't aware of the lack. But then, he came to be named Small Brother by Old Father, and then New One by Strong Spirit, and subsequently Stalker by Jack the Collier, until the time came when he finally named himself—Harry.

PART ONE
PRESENT DAY

I t's been a couple of months since Harry returned, and Elena and I have had a chance to adjust to him a bit more. He'd been gone for about five years, and for me, it's like meeting him all over again. I remember the first time I saw him when he was in his spider "configuration," and what a complete freak-out I had. At the time I had a severe spider phobia, and to say the beginning of the relationship was a little rocky is like saying the Himalayas are tall. To cap things off, Harry wasn't just your garden-variety spider—of course not— he was a *tarantula*, and an extraordinarily large one at that. Eventually I got over myself and was able to see Harry as a living, intelligent being, but still, definitely not human. Apparently not an extraterrestrial alien, either, but just between us it wouldn't surprise me at all to find out at some point that he actually *is* an alien. I mean, he's the first to say he doesn't remember everything in his past.

It's hard to imagine the apparently thousands and thousands of lives Harry has lived. He talks about what he refers to as his past lives, but it's not what we humans would normally understand as reincarnation. Harry doesn't die and get reborn into another body. Instead, he goes into what he describes as "stasis periods." When he comes out of each one, he says most of the time he'll have a new "configuration." He will have been in one bodily form when he conked out, and most usually, at least to some extent, a different bodily form— excuse me, configuration—when he wakes up. It seems that often the reconfigurations are pretty dramatic, like this most recent change. In spite of my initial phobia, I became very attached to Harry the Tarantula. But when he woke a few months ago and Elena found him in the back yard, he had changed into a completely different form. I still see mental images of his former tarantula configuration, and it's just crazy that now he's configured as very large Giant Asian Mantis. He can actually speak out loud now, *and fly*. He's also got these little mitten-type hands with actual thumbs. He's really excited about having thumbs. I'm going to go out on a limb here and show my squishy side—it's actually pretty adorable.

Harry says he's not exactly sure what triggers the stasis process, except for the times he's gotten critically injured and the process overtakes him. From what he's described, in some lives he's been injured so thoroughly that us humans wouldn't have been able to tell he wasn't clinically dead. Considering the thousands of epochs he's lived through, my guess is that *mostly dead* is the most obvious (and probably most frequent) stasis trigger, since he would have needed repairs to fix the mostly-dead parts in order to have future functionality. Since he's here now (we can have the subjective vs objective reality debate another time), it would appear he hasn't been completely dead yet, which seems beyond unrealistic if we were bringing reality into this discussion. Although, it occurs to me that if he was clinically dead at some point, would that necessarily mean that every single cell in whatever body he had at the time would have been dead, all at the same time? No life spark whatsoever? If even one cell remained alive, would that be enough to trigger stasis and re-life him? Harry doesn't remember enough to know one way or the other, and as I have zero related knowledge or training, I'm taking things at face value.

The stasis for the mostly-dead scenario doesn't give him much time to find a safe place to lie low for the duration of the incredibly long periods he's been in stasis. There are other times when he will become increasingly lethargic; he knows stasis is in-bound and has time to find a safe place to hunker down for a few millennia or so. Harry thinks the lethargy-based type of stasis may enable him to develop a deeper configuration to suit the next epoch he faces. Sometimes the stasis period can be much shorter, like this last five-year period. He was forced into stasis that time because he had expended every atom of his energy store to save the life of our elderly neighbor, Mrs. Gonzales. She had suffered a heart attack, and Harry somehow used his energy to act as a living defibrillator. I don't fully understand the mechanism he used, but he got her heart started, which kept her alive until the EMTs arrived. I had to go to the hospital with her, and when I got back Harry was gone and I didn't know where. He was gone for five years, a relatively long time to us humans, but a figurative eyeblink for Harry.

Elena is doing great with him, and he has a mighty crush on her. At first she had a couple of alien-brain-eating night-mares that took her a couple of days to get over. Like me, when she first heard Harry talking it was difficult for her to come to grips with Harry as a non-human being and not actually an insect at all. At first she thought she might be lying in a coma with a brain tumor and hallucinating like crazy. I assured her that was not the case, but then for a couple of hours she was suspicious of me and my friend Dan, and thought it was all a bizarre prank. It took several weeks for her to steady out and come to see Harry as I see him. She still gets sort of a bemused expression on her face whenever she's around him, though. She drove into work today and blew Harry a kiss as she went out the door. Speaking of, I have to get busy with today's work myself, so I head back to my "office," which is just a small desk and office chair, wedged in with miscellaneous stuff stored in the extra bedroom. On my way there, I stop in the living room beside Harry's aquarium and tap on the glass to get his attention.

"Hey pal, how'd you like to observe a master of technology at work today?"

Harry flits up to sit on the edge of his aquarium and looks at me questioningly. "I'd like that, but who are we going to observe?"

"You really know how to hurt a guy, Harry. I was talking about me. I thought you'd like to see up close what a modern workday looks like—you know, a non-human version of "Take Your Kid to Work Day." When you were here before I was still commuting to the office most weekdays. Things changed a lot while you were gone—remind me to tell you about a little thing we call the pandemic. During the quarantine I worked from home, like everyone else. That setup worked pretty well and now the company is letting people keep doing that, except for the occasional face-to-face meeting I can't weasel out of. I don't miss the daily drive time, I can tell you that. Come on, up you go."

I pat my shoulder, and Harry flies up and settles himself close to my ear. I pick up my coffee cup and walk down the hallway to my office. I flip the lights on, sit in my comfy swivel chair, and fire up my laptop. Harry drifts down to the desktop and gets up close to the laptop screen.

"You know you'll wreck your eyes getting that close to the screen. Back up a few steps."

Harry moves back one whole step and appears to be mesmerized by the wallpaper display of fish darting about a coral reef. "I've often wondered how is this different from a TV."

"I'm not sure it's all that different in terms of using the system for entertainment instead of work purposes. I guess you've seen that the everyday electronics most people use are all different kinds. Each kind supposedly has a primary use, but I'm not sure I believe that, at least for phones and laptops. For instance, I can make calls from my laptop, but if I want to chat with someone on the fly I'm going to use my phone to actually make a call. Not to show my age, but I think a lot of people use their phone just for social media. I mean, why talk when you can text, right?"

Harry nods, but I think he looks a little confused. I try to give a better explanation:

"Personally, I think it's more about how we use our various devices than the devices themselves. Unless of course you're Team Apple and have several mortgages to cover device upgrades. We can listen to music, watch movies or TV shows, and play games on the TV, this laptop, *and* my cell phone, pretty much whatever we want, whenever we want."

Harry moves back a couple more paces and watches closely as I use the keyboard to type in the laptop password. The home screen comes up, and I select my email icon. The app opens up and *voila*, there are a *lot* of emails waiting for me. I sigh and take a sip of coffee. I check the time and see that I can probably fool around a few more minutes before I have to dive in. Harry looks up at me with what I think is a hopeful expression.

"You mentioned listening to music? Is that something

that's difficult to arrange? I would love to be able to listen to music now and then, especially if you and Elena aren't home."

I could slap myself for being an idiot. "It's not difficult at all, Harry, and I'm sorry I didn't think of it myself. Let's go in the living room and I'll get it set up for you. Then I'll come back in here and get to work."

I have the phone in the pocket of my robe (no need for actual work clothes—pants—if you work from home, right?), and huff around while trying to get the phone charger detangled from everything else plugged into the power strip under the desk. The robe is not optimal wear for this task; it's actively fighting my knees. I'm a little out of breath after climbing under the desk and conclude that it wouldn't be a bad idea for me to get more exercise. Just a little more, no need to go crazy and join a gym or something. I wrap the long phone charger cord into loops around one hand and with my other, I gesture for Harry to climb aboard. We make our way back down the hall, but first I take a quick detour to the kitchen for a coffee refill. Harry declines, saying he's had enough caffeine for now.

Back in the living room, we get settled into the recliner, with Harry perched on the chair arm. I show him the control on the side of the phone and move the volume up and down so he can see how it works. I lower the volume again and put the phone flat on the chair arm. Harry flies down to sit beside it to try the volume control himself. I'm thinking he won't be able to move the toggle up and down, but to my surprise he manages to do it. I suspect his tiny mantis-arms are stronger than they appear to be.

"This is wonderful, Tristan! Would you be able to leave your phone out here with me while you work?"

I stand up and make sure the charger cord is out of the way. "Sure, that's no problem. If I need to make a call I'll just come out here and we'll share the phone."

I pick up my coffee and take a noisy slurp. "You build your playlist, and later you can show me what you put together."

Harry is engrossed with the phone and doesn't look up as I leave, but he waves a hand at me over his shoulder. I hear a couple of different songs start then stop as I meander back down the hallway to my office. I feel pretty pleased with myself that I've introduced Harry to the Digital Age.

H arry thought this was turning out to be a very good day. He was thrilled that he could listen to music using Tristan's phone and could even construct his own playlist. This was a freedom he hadn't known existed; in his imaginings he had not conceived that using an electronic device would be something he'd be able to do himself. He realized that "hands" could take a number of forms—it didn't have to be thumbs *and* fingers both; he thought he might not be as physically limited as he'd first appeared.

He skipped through dozens of songs, trying to find something that struck a chord with him, so to speak. Harry was listening to a song that seemed to be about someone whose truck had been taken by his woman, along with his heart, when he noticed an option labeled "Browse." He understood that "to browse" meant looking over a number of choices and wondered what sort of choices might be on offer. He found a sixties rock song that said to let the sound take him away, to look inside and see what he could find. YES, this was what he wanted! He started bobbing his head, pumping his arm in rhythm with the guitars and drums. He felt somehow that this just had to be louder and increased the volume. He almost forgot to add the song to his playlist but caught it in time. The song ended and he wanted more. The next song had Harry headed down the highway, born to be wild$_2$. He thought it was particularly applicable and saved that one too. He continued to bob his head and realized that he really must move more of his body than just his head. Unfortunately, he didn't know how to dance, so he just frantically waved his arms around and kicked his legs out from side to side, while still bobbing his head. It felt really good to move like this.

Harry stopped dancing when the song ended and went back to browsing. He chose 70s Rock Classics, and figuratively immigrated to a new land from the land of ice and snow$_3$. From there, he continued his rock journey to the Lake Geneva shoreline$_4$, saving everything to his playlist as he traveled the incredible landscape of sound issuing from the phone's speakers. He saw the Heavy Metal selection and donned his metaphorical black veil$_5$, which led him to find that he could play air guitar along with the wicked guitar riffs in the song. He noticed an option to change the bass level and cranked that up, then realized this wonderful music must be louder yet, and put the volume up as high as it would go. Harry had never known such music existed and lost himself in the world of pounding rhythms that rattled his tiny mantis teeth.

Back in his office, Tristan was absorbed in the blueprints for the current building project that he had brought up on-screen. He found himself unconsciously tapping his foot, bobbing his head, then a blast of sound nearly lifted him from his swivel chair. He realized what he was hearing and laughed —this music brought back some pretty wild memories. His music tastes of late had mellowed and definitely headed more out to the country variety of genres, but Tristan was still a little bit of a metal head from way back.

Harry's rock music metal fest lasted for over an hour before he was finally exhausted and had to take a break. He lowered the volume and searched for something more restful. He found a selection for Medieval Chants, wondering what that might be; he chose it and the room was filled with what seemed to be similar to the monastic chanting he had heard when he lived at the monastery with Brother Mark, back in medieval times. He felt a little shock when he realized the music currently playing actually was the same chant he'd heard the monk sing during services in the monastery's church. He adjusted the bass tone to a more reasonable level and lowered the volume again, then closed his eyes and lay down to rest beside the phone on the chair arm. He was drifting off when he remembered the other icons he'd seen when Tristan had started the phone. Since the music had been so good, Harry wondered what other fabulous things might the phone do?

Elena arrived home just then from her office in the city, and as she opened the front door she heard low voices singing what sounded like music she'd heard during mass at her mother's church. She shrugged out of her jacket and pitched it toward the coat rack standing in the entryway, then kicked off her shoes in the same direction with a relieved sigh and wandered into the living room. She could tell from the tantalizing aromas wafting from the kitchen that Tristan had started dinner. She noticed Harry waving to her from the chair arm. He exited the music app and the low, relaxing music stopped in mid-chant.

"Elena, guess what! Tristan showed me how to use his phone to stream music."

"Really? That's good. I listen to music on my phone sometimes while I'm at work. Did he show you anything else you could do with a phone?"

Harry rubbed his head and blinked his large eyes at Elena. "Well, I know it's used to make actual phone calls, but I don't know much more than that."

Elena continued through the living room and popped her head into the kitchen to let Tristan know she was home, then came back and sat in the recliner next to Harry. She picked up the phone, pulling the charger free and letting it fall back to the floor. She put the recliner footrest up and comfortably settled back. Harry flit-hopped up to sit on her shoulder, marveling at how her manner with him had relaxed in the past few weeks. He thought her hair smelled like sunshine and that Elena was, in general, pretty wonderful. She smiled warmly at Harry, and he felt an odd sensation of lightness; he'd have to ask Tristan about that effect.

"In that case, let me show you a couple of other fun things you might like. Do you remember when you first came back and I took your picture? I'll show you where I posted it. You know what an icon is, right? Okay, so this one is for Instagram. When I took your picture, I put it on my Instagram account on my phone so my friends could see you, my new friend. I've been so busy I haven't checked my account for a while. I can access it from Tristan's phone, so let's take a look."

Elena logged on to her Instagram account and scrolled to the picture she had taken the day she found him in the garden, under the blueberry bush. She navigated to the post with Harry's picture, then noticed the number of followers and what looked like a few dozen comments.

"Huh. Look at this, Harry. It looks like you're a popular guy. Let's go show Tristan."

She made sure Harry was stable on her shoulder, then put the recliner footrest down and stood, still looking at the display on the phone. She tapped on the screen as she walked into the kitchen. Tristan was standing at the stove, concentrating on stirring something that was simmering in a large pot set on a low heat. He looked up as Elena and Harry entered and noticed that she seemed a bit more animated than was usual for the end of a workday. She waved the phone at him to show the display and handed the device to him.

"Tristan, look at this. That photo of Harry I posted has had a bunch of likes and comments."

Tristan stopped stirring to look closely at the photo, which had captured Harry straight-on with his head tilted to the side, looking quizzically at the camera lens. He immediately thought that there was no way Harry resembled a regular bug; his posture was very un-buglike, and his bright eyes clearly indicated intelligence. He started to have a funny feeling somewhere in his stomach.

"Uh, Elena, don't you think this could be a problem? It looks pretty clear to me that our little terrestrial alien here isn't just another pretty bug."

There was a whirring sound as Harry left Elena's shoulder to float in for a landing on the kitchen counter, looking aggrieved, arms crossed. "I don't understand why I have to keep saying this, Tristan. I'm not *any* kind of alien."

Tristan looked at him and raised an eyebrow. "Relax, pal." He gestured between himself and Elena. "*We* know that, but what if someone else doesn't? I'm just saying this is new territory for all of us and we need to understand it before we all decide it's just fucking wonderful."

Elena frowned. "First of all, cursing. Second, unless someone *believed* Harry was an alien—no offense, Harry—he honestly does look like a Giant Asian Mantis. Scientists are finding new species almost every day, and I'm pretty sure their first thought is not that the new thing is an alien."

Harry sniffed in a decidedly snippy manner. "For what it's worth, I agree with Elena. I look perfectly normal now, for a specified value of Giant Asian Mantis normal."

Tristan sat down at the kitchen table, which was already set for dinner, Harry's china included. He sighed and rubbed his eyes. "Listen, both of you. I understand what you're saying. What *I'm* saying is that we love Harry and Harry loves us. Our perspectives are not completely clear when it comes to what other people might think of him."

Elena sat down at the table and Harry flitted over from the countertop to join them. Elena patted Tristan's hand. "I understand, Tristan, but I honestly don't think you

need to worry. Let's look through the comments while we eat and then we'll have an idea of what people do think of him." She smiled at Harry and he felt light again. "And yes, we all do love Harry."

Tristan nodded distractedly and stood. "Food's ready anyway, so let's eat and figure this out."

After they had all been served and began eating, Elena placed the phone on the table beside her plate. "Okay, let's see what we have here. I'll read some out loud to get a feel for how people are leaning." She grinned at Harry. "You know, Team Alien or Team Bug."

Tristan snorted and Harry rolled his eyes. Satisfied, Elena navigated to the comments and began looking through them. She took a bite of food and chewed slowly while she read.

"Okay, so there are a couple dozen likes so far. Harry, that literally means just that someone liked your picture. I'm paging down through the first few comments, which are either 'So cool!' or just 'Wow.' A friend asks where did I find it. Sorry, Harry, there are also a few 'Ewws' as well, but don't worry about that. Some people are afraid of everything."

She continued eating and Harry and Tristan went back to

their own dinners. Tristan had been trying out various vegetarian meals, and this one was pretty good. Harry was enjoying his food when he noticed Elena looked a little worried herself. Tristan had caught it as well and raised an eyebrow.

"Is there someone who might not be thinking Harry is 'so cool'"?

Elena swallowed another bite before answering. "Not exactly. Remember how I said scientists are finding new species every day? There are a couple of comments here where the person says Harry belongs to a new species and wants to come see Harry for themselves."

Tristan snorted. "Well, obviously that's not going to happen. Is the photo geo-tagged?"

Elena looked a little more worried. "Yes, unfortunately. I always forget geo-tagging is on unless it's disabled in the settings. What if someone shows up here?"

Tristan picked up his plate and set it in the sink. "Let's let the dishes go for now and take a look at some more comments."

Elena made a pot of tea while Tristan and Harry wandered into the living room and got settled into their usual spots. She carried in a small tea tray and set it on the end table beside the couch, then poured the tea into two big mugs and several drops into a miniature china cup, handing them off to Tristan and Harry. She sat on the end of the couch beside the table, lifted her own mug and took a couple of small sips before retrieving her phone from her pocket. She navigated to the Instagram comments, quickly scrolling through them to get back to the one from the person who wanted to see Harry. She paused to read it out loud:

"Thank you for posting your photo of such a magnificent specimen of insect. I haven't seen anything like that during the years I've spent forming my own insect information archive. I hope to meet with you soon to see it for myself if that would be possible. Please reply to me via email at...."

Elena's voice trailed off and she looked over at Tristan with a frown. "Kind of quirky here. I don't know what they mean by an 'insect information archive.' Maybe they don't know about Wikipedia, although I'd find that hard to believe. I had expected the email address to be associated with a university somewhere, but this looks like a personal account on a service I don't recognize."

Tristan took a long, noisy slurp of his tea, finishing it off. "I guess quirky isn't necessarily bad, but it depends on the degree of quirky. In this case, I don't see the harm in just asking to see Harry. You're going to refuse, right?" He lifted his eyebrows and looked at Elena over the rim of the mug he still held at his chin.

"Of course. It would be foolish to invite a complete stranger to our home and take a chance with Harry's well-being. I'm going to respond to his comment to decline a visit, but I'm not sending an email."

Tristan placed his mug on the floor beside him and stretched out in the recliner. "Well, unless there's another comment that implies a SWAT team is coming in, let's watch a movie. I'm in the mood for big explosions."

Elena rolled her eyes. "As if you're ever in the mood for anything else. It's a good thing I like big explosions, too. Hey, Harry—how about you?"

Harry had been tense during the comments discussion, and with a sigh, he let himself relax. "I *love* big explosions! And monsters! At the same time!"

CHAPTER THREE

Several more months had now passed since Harry's return. The household had found its rhythm and a semblance of daily, familial routine was developing. Through Harry's shared memories, Elena was gradually coming to understand Harry's existence, as much as she felt a rational person could even begin to understand it. To Tristan it seemed that Elena and Harry were developing an unexpected closeness. Tristan loved his biological family, of course, but over the years he had unintentionally become distant from them. Phone calls took the place of visits, texts took the place of phone calls.

Pre-Harry, Tristan would not have thought about feelings —there was too much interference from football and beer. When Tristan looked back at the gruff construction engineer he had been, he thought that guy might have been lonely. Then Elena moved in and later Harry came back, and most of the time Tristan felt like he had been granted a whole fistful of wishes. He had everything he loved within his grasp, but in the depths of night he feared that if he wasn't careful, it could somehow all disappear, like mist rising to meet the sun. The fear of loss was much more visceral to him than any loneliness he had denied. Regardless, each day deceptively ran its course of calm routine. The new little family pretended to be normal, for a given value of the current, accepted human form of normal.

For himself, Harry couldn't recall a time when his conscious life had been as safe and comfortable, for such an extended period, as it was now with Tristan and Elena. Time that he would have spent foraging, running for his life, or hiding was now his to fill with other activities. He had the luxury of being cared for, so that he could think about and do other things. So, on one particular day, he sat in his aquarium and considered what to do with himself. The house was quiet, as both Elena and Tristan had had to go into their city offices that morning. It was mid-afternoon by then, and the usual Friday evening commuter traffic hadn't yet hit the road in front of the house. The only sound Harry could hear was the ticking of the heirloom clock Elena had brought with her to hang on a living room wall.

Harry groomed his wings for the third time in the past hour. He fussily rearranged a few pieces of bedding in his aquarium and dusted off his plastic palm tree, then flitted into the kitchen and sat on the counter for a few minutes, just looking around. As always, the kitchen was clean and tidy, the counters clear of the various small appliances that seemed to aggregate around humans. He flitted into the air and chased a few dust motes, then flew back to the living room and sat on the couch arm for a few minutes, looking around in there. He felt tense and unhappy, itchy and edgy, and was hungry in spite of having finished the lunch Elena had left out for him before going to work. He was frustrated and irritably wondered what was wrong with him. Feeling at odds like this was new to him.

Harry was bored.

He flitted back into the kitchen and stood on the windowsill above the sink, looking outside to the back yard. The weather was gloomy and wet, and the garden was already prepared for what passed for winter in the South. He turned from the window and hopped down to the counter where earlier he had spied a phone lying face up, with a charger cord plugged into one end. The other end of the charger cord was attached to a blocky thing plugged into an electrical outlet situated on the wall in back of and to the left of the sink. It was a standard home outlet, with a place to plug in a power cord and a couple of simple on/off switches to run things from the outlet. The long charger cord had been roughly bundled into a few loops which had been pushed back, along with the flat, rectangular phone, to where the wall met the counter. Harry assumed this placement was to avoid the chance of the phone accidentally falling into the sink, since he understood that water and electronics were usually incompatible. Other than that, he didn't know much about plumbing. Not being able to manage human tools, he had once been the designated observer while Elena acted as the tool- and flashlight-holding assistant as Tristan fixed a leak under the sink. Tristan was an accomplished handyman, but Harry had learned some new words that day, which Elena made clear were not to be repeated by Harry, and preferably not by Tristan either.

Taking a closer look, he saw that it was Elena's phone, and he realized she had forgotten it in her rush to leave for work that morning. It should have been hard to miss, as the counters were completely clean and clear, but still, there it lay. Harry walked to the end of the windowsill and jumped down to land on the counter near the phone. The phone screen was dark, but

Elena had shown him how to "wake it up." He tapped sharply in the middle of the screen and the display lit up, showing a place to enter a password, which he tapped in. He had watched from her shoulder when Elena changed her password to match the date she had found Harry in the garden. Harry's day-to-day memory was prodigious and infallible, essentially recording all data that came to his awareness. Remembering a simple password was inconsequential, and he soon had access to all the apps and data on Elena's phone. Elena had shown Harry how to do a lot of different things on the phone, so that he could learn more about the world he now inhabited. Harry was fascinated with the idea of being in touch with so many people in so many different ways— photos, videos, music—the list seemed endless.

Harry knew much of what was on the phone would be private, but he thought Elena wouldn't mind if he looked through some of her Instagram posts again. After all, she had already shown them to him a few times. He'd never tried to do access Instagram on his own, but it had looked pretty easy when Elena did it. He navigated through the proper series of icons and menu selections to open the app and access her posts. He wanted to see if his photo had gotten any more likes or comments; the last time they had checked, the likes were almost up to a hundred. It was hard for him to imagine that almost a hundred people had seen his image. Harry thought that was probably the most people who had ever seen him, all at once so to speak, in the course of one lifetime. Elena thought the post still had possibilities of going fully viral and wanted to see how it played out. Tristan thought the tone of the comments hadn't gotten all the way to crazy town yet, but he recommended they all stay wary and circumspect. Harry still wasn't completely sure what "going viral" meant, but at this point the postings apparently didn't seem dangerous. There weren't many new comments. The quirky, wanna-be entomologist, whom Tristan had creatively dubbed Critter Gitter (just Critter for short), still cropped up a couple of times a week. Critter had started posting photos of other forms of praying mantis, trying to find one that matched Harry, while also continuing to obsessively beg for Elena's participation in their quest to identify Harry.

Harry perched on the phone, completely engrossed in reading the new comments on the small screen display, when just then a call came through. Elena hadn't found a ringtone she liked and had set her phone to both vibrate and buzz, at full volume, rather than ring for incoming calls. She had also set those alerts to go on for a very long time to be sure she heard them and could get to the phone in time to answer it. The sudden shock of the extremely loud, thrumming noise, along with the deep rumbling under his feet, caused Harry's fight-or-flight reflex to send him vaulting backward into the air, catching himself at a hover just above the counter. He had unintentionally used all four of his legs to push off from the phone, which was enclosed in a hard plastic case and lying on a hard surface, all of which combined to send the phone in a fast slide across the smooth countertop, away from the wall and toward the sink. Harry watched with horror as the ongoing vibrations caused the phone to skitter even closer to the sink, dragging the long charging cord behind it. As the sink was mounted from below, there was no flange edge around it that could possibly stop the phone's progress. Harry panicked; even though there was no water in the sink at the moment, the sink was where water *went*. Water belonged in the sink—the phone did not. He had to keep the phone from harm, but as usual, time to plan was non-existent. He could only follow his instincts, along with whatever past experiences he could remember under stress.

The continuing buzz and clattering vibrations, which were causing the phone to progressively twitch across the counter, were also making Harry's ears throb. He impulsively descended from his hover low enough to grab the charger cord a few inches from where it connected to the phone. Harry's largely unformed plan of the moment was to use the cord to gently remove the phone from imminent danger. He thought that lifting it up a little and gradually drawing it away (like using a crane) would be easier than trying to pull its dead weight, lying flat, across the counter. Holding firmly onto the cord, Harry flitted his wings and slowly ascended up and back while the phone continued to violently twitch at the end of the cord. The connected end of the phone sluggishly rose below Harry as he gained altitude, but he wasn't getting much forward movement from the end of the phone still resting on the counter. He continued to slowly rise and gently pull and managed to lift the connected end of the phone just enough to see a few centimeters of space between it and the counter, but the unconnected end still merely twitched in place. Having previously learned what could happen when one didn't account for reactions to one's own actions, especially when pulling on cords, he was very careful in applying a little extra force to the charger cord in order to also move the non-elevated end of the phone.

Harry was much stronger than he appeared, but the weight of the phone was nearly too much for him. His arms began to tremble with the strain of keeping the phone lifted while attempting to draw it away from the sink. He desperately flitted his wings faster to remain aloft while the phone continued to vibrate and skitter. However, with one end of the phone lifted, instead of the energy of the vibration transfer-ring downward and dispersing throughout the countertop, some now traveled instead upward through the cord. Harry felt like he was gripping a buzzing snake. Mercifully, just then the call either went to voice mail or the caller hung up, and the vibrations stopped.

Unfortunately, the charger cord was an older one, and the metal end connecting to the phone was worn. The connection was far from snug in the best of circumstances; the combined effects of Harry pulling on the cord, along with the vibration-caused twitching, had caused the metal end to become even more loosely connected. As tended to happen with many of Harry's endeavors, events were set in motion. Just as he drew in a relieved breath and had the passing thought that things were going unusually well, the connector came free from the phone and the phone fell back onto the counter with a loud clacking sound, lying at an angle with a corner too near the sink edge for comfort. Harry yelled one of the plumbing words he had learned from Tristan and threw the cord down in frustrated disgust.

CHAPTER FOUR

Harry was no longer bored.

He settled onto the counter and rubbed some feeling back into his hands, which had gone numb from holding the vibrating cord. Although it seemed that the situation was under control for the moment, Harry didn't trust it to stay that way. He narrowed his eyes, thinking it was quiet —*too* quiet. He knew that if this were a horror movie, the villain, whether zombie, vampire, or your standard axe murderer, would be hiding around the corner, ready to leap out while wielding the death-dealing implement each appropriate to its user. He chose not to be fooled by the supposedly sleeping phone and decided he had to try something else to move it back to its original place against the wall, far away from the blasted sink.

Harry warily approached the phone to determine how he could best go about moving it, immensely grateful it was quiet and no longer twitching. He positioned himself at the corner of the phone closest to the sink and gave the phone a gentle, tentative push away from himself, toward the wall. The phone in its hard plastic case did seem to move more easily while flat on the counter (and not twitching), but its mass was bulky and unwieldy to manage. Harry could have smacked himself for not trying to simply push it in the first place, but the twitching had been formidable. Although his small push had moved the phone only a very tiny measure, he was encouraged that the phone had moved at all. Harry believed in "more is better": the phone would move farther and more easily if pushed harder. He backed away a few steps and launched a ground assault, thinking to generate momentum that would propel the phone right where he wanted it to go. He used his forward thrust to give the nearest corner of the phone as hard a push toward the wall as he could manage. He wanted to get it moving away from the sink as quickly as possible, but he had never been one to calculate angles and trajectories.

The physics of applying such sharp-force thrust to a corner, rather than using a sustained directional push on the middle of a side and adjusting for drift, immediately showed effect. Harry was learning a lot about the application of different levels of energy to an object and the object's reaction to that applied energy. In his experience, such reactions usually had unintended, not to mention unexpected, results. He shouldn't have been surprised, then, when the phone went into a fast, tight spin, catching him across two of his four ankles. The impact put him off balance and when he fell, the still-spinning phone caught him on his side and sent him sliding on his back into the wall. He came to rest behind the faucet mounted at the back of the sink. Fate being what it is, the phone came to rest teetering back and forth on the edge of the sink. Harry's horror and panic could only increase as he watched the phone tip downward, seemingly in slow motion, to slide down into the large, deep sink, coming to rest sticking halfway up out of the drain. Harry's vision swam with spots, and he felt faint. He shook his head to clear it but otherwise didn't move. He needed a minute to think.

After a few seconds he stood, knees a little shaky, and limped over to stand beside the faucet. He leaned his left arm on the faucet for support and carefully bent over to look down into the sink. It was a long way down to the bottom of the sink, where the phone had come to rest in the drain in an upright position, tilted at a jaunty angle. It appeared to rest comfortably on some sort of flat, rubbery material barely visible below the rim of the drain. The rubbery material had two slits cut in a cross on it, and the angle of the phone had pushed sections of the material downward, like a flower opening in reverse. It was clearly obvious the phone was still in danger. Harry feared he would never be able to wrangle the stupid thing to safety on his own. He sighed when he concluded he had no option other than to try pulling it out somehow, well before Tristan and Elena got home. He needed a plan and he needed materials. His saw that his only immediately available option was to try using the charger cord to drag the phone out of the drain, up from the sink, and onto the counter.

Since the phone wasn't in motion at the moment,

Harry didn't feel immediately pressed for time. He took a moment for a quick, calming groom, then ambled over to check on the condition of the connector. When the phone had dropped from aloft, the connector had gotten bent and now looked like a sort of flat hook at the end of the cord. Harry picked up the cord by the bent connector, and gripping it tightly (thumbs!), he used it to gently pull on the cord to straighten it out. This action triggered a random memory of sweet pea tendrils, but he brushed that aside. He then let that end drop to the counter, and disconsolately trudged alongside the length of the charger cord back where it hung from the blocky thing plugged into the wall outlet. The overall cord was lengthy, but because one end of it was connected to the block, it was held just a bit too short for Harry's current need.

Harry thought it would be much easier to pull the phone up out of the sink if the cord wasn't attached to the block at the other end. He could see where the cord disappeared into the bottom of the block and thought it would be a simple matter to disconnect the two. He firmly placed his mittens on the cord right where it connected to the block, and using all his strength, pulled down on it as hard as he could.

Instead of the end of the cord coming free of the block, the block pulled free of the outlet, hitting Harry's shoulder and bouncing off his front left foot before clattering to a stop on the counter. Harry hopped and staggered while expressing his fury using more plumbing words. That the block was out of the outlet wasn't necessarily a problem, but one never knew how the ripple effect of the unexpected results of applied energy would turn out. As well, consideration of the weight of things wasn't usually something Harry included in his plans. Here and now, as in some past adventures, Harry failed to consider the weight of the phone, just as he always over-estimated his own strength.

Harry remembered his near-fatal escape from the crows during his first time with Tristan, and therefore planned his next steps very carefully: First, make sure there was enough length to drag the bent-hook end of the cord down into the sink; second, wrap the cord around the phone a few times; and third, tie the cord tightly in place so that it stayed on the phone. He would then go back to end connected to the block and pull the cord, mitten over mitten, to drag the phone up out of the sink and back onto the counter. He would then carefully and slowly *push* the phone back to its original place under the wall outlet.

The block made pulling and maneuvering the charger cord more challenging, primarily due to its extra weight, but after considerable effort Harry had gotten the untidy loops of cord gathered at the sink's edge. He paused a moment to catch his breath, looking down into the depths of the sink. It was still a long way down to the bottom. Glancing up through the window, Harry could see more clouds moving in, further darkening an already gray day to make the overall ambience of his situation even more sinister. As the light coming through the window dimmed, he felt an anxious qualm— more than a qualm, really, since he could feel his wings shivering. Resolutely, Harry decided to take his chances with karma, and he soldiered on, whispering encouragement to himself: *"Do—or do not. There is no try."*

Harry stepped around to the back the large pile of looped cord where it lay waiting for his next move. He wasn't normally one to anthropomorphize inanimate objects, but he had a vague impression that the cord was mocking him, daring him to take action. Based on his recollections of his past experiences, he had previously concluded that cords were not his friends, but his options here were worse than limited. Harry decided that he would not let *this* cord get the better of him. Taking another deep breath, he bent over as much as he could, given his current configuration, and began pushing the loops over the edge of the sink.

Harry could have benefited from paying more attention to the worksite safety lectures he remembered Tristan telling him about. Or, failing that, he could have replayed in his memory any episode of his favorite Alaska king crab fishing show where the deck boss was screaming at the greenhorns to keep their feet planted on the deck and *watch out! watch out!* for the coils of rope being thrown over the side. Admittedly, the king crab situation was far more deadly than Harry's current situation, but in this he was the greenhorn learning the proverbial ropes. Distracted by his anxiety for the phone's welfare, he didn't recall either of those helpful scenarios. Consequently, he inadvertently stepped inside the last loop of the cord as he watched the rest of it slithering away, falling into the sink loop by loop. A loop sliding past him banged into his hurt foot and he awkwardly lifted it out of the way, only to have the last loop snare an ankle. Harry was pulled off balance and fell onto his side, kicking frantically to free his ankle as he went overboard into the sink. In this cord episode, though, he landed on top of the looped heap and not under it. As well, he didn't have an audience of crows to worry about. He landed hard on his back and his breath whooshed out of him; he could feel a back leg and the end of one wing crumple.

By this point, Harry was weary but didn't feel he

could give up. There was still a chance he could prevail over circumstances, although his odds seemed to be dwindling. He sat dispiritedly atop the cord heap and reviewed his options. After a few moments to recover, he stood and began inspecting his various injuries. His ankle was well and truly wrenched, and his foot throbbed in time with his heartbeat. His shoulder ached. He could fully extend one wing, but the other, crumpled as it was, would come out only halfway. Flying was still pretty new to Harry, but he suspected it would be difficult to fly properly with a damaged wing, and his ability to fly was crucial to rescuing the phone. He eyed the cord where it draped over the sink edge. Since the other end was not secured, he couldn't risk putting his weight on it to climb out of the sink; he had to be able to fly out. He gingerly extended his good wing and twitched it to ensure he could control it. The other wing he extended as far as it could go, which was about halfway;

reaching beyond that caused a hot bolt of pain to flash through his wing muscles. He gave a thought to being glad that it was just the wing muscles that were injured, and that the wing itself was not damaged beyond a few wrinkles. He pulled the injured wing back until the pain was tolerable, then twitched both as he normally would to gain altitude. The result was far from satisfactory.

H arry had watched any number of movies that included spectacular helicopter crashes. He had observed that the percentage of survivable crashes was directly related to how well the pilot could keep the damaged rotors going as the aircraft fell out of the sky. He had had a few nightmares where he woke himself yelling "*pull up, pull up*!!" The inherent problem now was that, while helicopters generally crashed either down or sideways, Harry would have to somehow crash *up* in order to return to the counter. While he mused on that issue, he grasped the bent end of the cord and began limping clockwise around the phone, dragging the largely unwieldy cord behind him. Luckily, the pile of loops unraveled from the top as he pulled them out. He was too physically and emotionally worn out to berate himself for being in this situation in the first place and gave his concentration to enwrapping the phone. Not having a watch that would fit his mantis wrist, Harry didn't know how long it took him to finally be able to fashion a knot to keep the cord on the phone. He checked out the window again and saw that the sky was much darker; it seemed more time had passed than he thought, and his family would be home soon. He had little time remaining to finish up and could feel anxious palpitations begin to pulse through his body.

Finally, Harry was ready to send himself aloft. He gave the knotted cord one last tug and saw that it was secure. He stepped away from the phone, closer to the shining, vertical cliff wall that was the vast side of the sink. Looking up and up, his heart sank a little, but he was determined to prevail. He extended his good wing, then pushed past the pain and forced the injured wing muscles to fully extend that wing as well. He twitched both wings and his feet lifted from the ground. He clenched his jaw and twitched his wings harder and faster, then taking a running jump, wobbled into the air. With each dip of his wings he pushed himself higher, riding the pain, until he reached the top of the sink-cliff wall. His eyesight was blurry from stress and fatigue, and as he shook his head he realized he needed to move not just up, but over as well. He had to land, preferably not back in the bottom of the sink. He gave one more tremendous effort to move laterally, and saw the counter come under his feet as he lost consciousness. As he faded out, he thought *"any landing you can walk away from is a good landing."*

When Harry regained his senses, he found himself back where he had started earlier in the day. He staggered to his feet and leaned against the wall beside the block where it still lay on the counter, directly under the switches on the wall outlet. He was enjoying a brief rest, readying himself for his next effort in saving the phone, but his plan to pull it out of the sink seemed overwhelming, and he began to doubt he could do it.

Suddenly the phone began to buzz and vibrate again with another inbound call, the vibrations causing it to wildly shimmy in the drain. The metal drain acted as an amplifier for both the noise of the vibration and the clanging of the phone against the interior of the drain. The horrendous noise badly startled Harry, causing him to jump straight up in fear. He hit the top of his head on the underside of one of the switches, flipping it up. The horrendous noise immediately became a scream like that of a tortured jet engine. There was a horrible grinding noise added to the din. The phone was spinning wildly in the drain, which caused the remainder of the cord to wrap around it as it rapidly spun. As more of the cord wrapped around the phone, the end still attached to the block began to slide toward the sink.

The block slithered past Harry, headed for the devouring drain. Harry had no thought for himself and threw his body on the block as it flew past him, desperately trying to plant his feet in order to drag the block back from the sink, with the desperate hope of getting everything to just slow the hell down. The cord thinned and stretched; he could now see only the top part of the phone as it spun in the drain. He could also see blue sparks flashing inside the drain, down in the dark below the phone. Harry's little mantis-hands and little mantis-arms weren't up to the herculean requirements of the situation, and the block was torn from his grasp. The release of tension caused the block to snap into the air, then it hit the faucet handle and was caught. This did not deter the devouring drain, which continued to eat the remainder of the phone. The cord continued wrapping itself around the phone as it spun in the drain, while the block remained caught on the faucet handle. The resulting tension on the cord didn't pull the connector end of the cord from the block, as one might expect to happen. Instead, it pulled the faucet handle forward, turning on the water.

The house lights flickered, and the drain died with a

shrieking hiss when the water struck it. The noise stopped abruptly. There were a few more blue sparks, but then those died as well. Harry stood beside the sink in glassy-eyed shock, not fully comprehending all that had occurred. The sink was slowly filling with water, since the wreckage of the phone was now blocking the drain, but it wouldn't be long before a water-fall would hit the floor. Finally the smoke and electrical stench coming from the dead drain became too much for him. In despair, he walked to the edge of the counter and jumped off, trying to snap his wings out to slow his descent, but due to his injuries this was only minimally successful, and he landed hard on the kitchen floor. He was numb and couldn't think. He saw a dark, dusty little area beside the stove and crawled as far back into the darkness as he could. He shook for a long time, but eventually exhaustion took his awareness as the water slowly edged toward him.

"Hey, Harry, we're home..."

Just as I push the door open I smell something odd, like ozone and burned wiring. I've smelled that odor before, right before something caught fire. We can hear water running and when no one has been home who could turn the water on, that's never a good sound. I put on a hustle, Elena right behind me, and we quickly head to the kitchen. When we reach it we slip a little, going sideways across the wet floor, and have to grab onto a couple of chairs to stay upright. Water is still pouring out of the sink onto the floor, so that needs to stop. I slide over to the sink and turn the faucet off. As I'm turning the handle, I look down into the water-filled sink. Elena comes up beside me and leans over for a closer look.

"Is that my phone?"

After being coaxed out of his hiding place, Harry had given Tristan and Elena a play-by-play review of the death of the phone. They said they *really* wished they could have seen the whole episode. Harry thought their not-so-hidden amusement was terrifically unsympathetic and felt a little surly about it. Since Harry couldn't remember a time when he had been a member of an actual family, Tristan and Elena had explained that families can come in all sorts of combinations, some of which include very much loved non-human members. Harry learned that family members can be forgiven the occasional mistake, like feeding someone's phone to the garbage disposal. He also learned about cloud backups and device insurance. Harry's extreme upset was alleviated; in fact, the next day, when Elena brought him an exciting, unexpected present.

Elena gave Harry his very own cell phone. He wasn't sure what "BOGO" meant, other than Elena was pretty happy about it and talked a lot about how smart it was to have insured their phones in the first place, despite the extra cost. Apparently, it worked out that she hadn't had to pay anything for either phone, which Harry understood was "a *really* great deal". While the exact parameters that constituted a *really* great deal appeared to be infinitely variable, Harry knew it was something both she and Tristan regularly strived to achieve when obtaining things the family needed. After Harry had unwrapped his present, there was some considered family discussion of data usage. Elena mentioned gaming, in a not completely positive manner, which Tristan claimed was unfair. Elena also had a lot to say about Harry's "screen time," as opposed to him actually moving around getting exercise.

Harry hadn't lived under family rules before but decided this was a trade-off he was willing to make.

After dinner, Tristan set up the phone in Harry's aquarium so that it rested, longways, in a small plastic bracket mounted flat on the glass of one end of the rectangular tank, much like the flat screen TV was mounted on a living room wall. The phone's charging cord was connected to the phone and draped over the back glass plate of the aquarium, so that the charging block could be plugged into the outlet behind the table on which the aquarium stood, in its customary place below the window.

Harry repositioned his plastic palm tree and air fern and made himself a little sitting area where he could watch videos on the phone, but not be too close to the screen. He was so excited by all this it made his head feel a little swimmy. After plugging the charger into the outlet, Tristan plopped down onto the floor beside the table and sat with his legs crossed. Elena had already customized the phone for Harry's preferences, and when Harry turned it on now, the icons for all his favorite apps displayed on the screen.

Elena stepped back and waved her hand in a *ta-da* motion. "There you go, Harry. You now have your very own home entertainment and communication center. Go ahead and try it out." She gracefully sat cross-legged on the floor beside Tristan, and they both watched him maneuver through a few menus. Harry soon selected a movie from one of the several streaming services. He stepped back from his new "wall display" and watched the credits beginning scrolling down the screen. He flitted up to the edge of the aquarium and bowed to Tristan and Elena.

"Lady and gentleman, in honor of the first time Tristan and I watched a movie together, I present for your entertainment, the first Mantis Home Theater showing of that science fiction classic, *Godzilla!*" He started to go back to his living room, then stopped and said over his shoulder, "It's the good one with Matthew Broderick, not the one with the tiny fairies."

PART TWO

PRESENT DAY

Their Saturday Night Movie feature had been a lot of fun, but now it was late, and all the house lights were off. Tristan and Elena had been asleep for several hours. As the nighttime hours counted down, the house became even more still, entering into what Harry thought of as its dark-time personality. Now was the time when known items cast shadows that seemed otherworldly, and time seemed to move more slowly. The night deepened further as Harry stood looking through the window under which his aquarium rested, and watched the full moon move across the sky. He didn't feel tired and wondered again how it was that his new configuration didn't seem to need much sleep. He had the usual anxious little twinge about how not sleeping might drain his energy more quickly. Harry wasn't sure how long it might take his new collectors to obtain a full charge, but if his memory of past-life experiences were an indication, he despaired of ever being able to fully recharge. He wondered how it would feel to have that much power, a truly full charge, at hand or rather at mitten.

Harry heard a small, rustling noise and turned from the window to look into the shadowed living room. He didn't see anything there that seemed out of place. The rustle came again, a little louder, and he turned back in time to see a large shadow move *outside* the window. He watched as the window frame rose silently, just two or three inches; it stopped, then rose a couple more. Harry was trying to decide if he was imagining things, and whether he should be frightened rather than curious, when something small and white was tossed through the window to land in the aquarium beside him. It looked soft and fluffy, like a minuscule cloud. Harry stepped closer to it for a better look and smelled a sharp, odd odor he didn't like. He began to feel very strange—dizzy and a little sick. His knees and legs weakened suddenly, and as he collapsed he thought he'd better go ahead and lie down for a minute, just until he could figure out what was going on.

A lone dark figure, an intruder, stood outside the open window, intently looking through it into the aquarium. The intruder saw Harry slump down and quickly used their watch to set a ten-second countdown. The time seemed more like ten minutes to them, and they nervously looked around the area to make sure they weren't being overtly watched. The light from the full moon in the cloudless sky provided an illumination the intruder had hoped to avoid. This window was on the side of the house and less visible from the street, but there was always a chance of discovery and the intruder's actions were obviously illegal. Being driven by obsession, the intruder chose to disregard that aspect of the current adventure. They returned to the timer, counting along as it proceeded to zero, at which point they clicked it off. Turning back to the window, the intruder placed gloved hands underneath the bottom of the frame, and very slowly raised it again so that it was now half-open. The plan had been to simply grab the insect and depart, but it was too dark within the house to see exactly where it was in the aquarium. There was no more time.

This was an older house, and the windows were long and narrow, with the bottom of the exterior window frame only two feet or so from the ground. The slightly built intruder wasn't tall, but they easily reached through the open window and grasped the rectangular aquarium with a hand on each end, then lifted it through the window and placed it on the damp ground beside their feet. Standing upright, they turned back to the window and drew it down, very quietly, until it was once more fully closed. They stood motionless for a few seconds, listening for any alarms. Their breathing was panicky from stress and their exhalations were visible in the cool night air. With an effort they clamped their lips together to eliminate even that visibility. It was unusually quiet; there were no frogs or crickets sounding at this chilly time of year.

Satisfied that nothing was moving other than the clouds finally coming in to block the moonlight, they picked up the aquarium and stealthily moved along the side of the house. Walking on the grass beside the driveway to avoid the crunchy gravel, the intruder quickly walked beside the driveway, then down the street to their car. They carefully placed the aquarium on the passenger seat, then closed the door on that side and went around to the driver's side. Within five minutes of closing the window, the intruder was heading to the freeway and home, a mere thirty minutes' drive away. The intruder impatiently pushed back the hood of the black sweat-shirt and distractedly rubbed a hand through the messy curls on their head. A quick glance in the rearview mirror showed a sweating, dark face with wide, frightened, dark green eyes. Now that the break-in was accomplished and they hadn't been caught, the adrenaline began to ebb and the shaking begin.

Harry felt a sharp pain in his flying muscles as his wing was carefully pulled out to the side. Seconds later, he felt another, much sharper pain in the middle of the wing itself. Before he could decide what he wanted to do about that pain, the two pains were repeated on his other side. His thoughts were muddled and he couldn't avoid drifting out of consciousness again. Before all thinking was gone and his mind shut down again, he saw the lights go off and felt a draft of air cross his body as a door was closed somewhere past him.

Some time later, Harry woke a second time. He was confused as to where he was currently located, since this didn't seem to be his aquarium. He realized he was lying facedown on some sort of board, with his wings spread out wide to either side. His legs felt a little crunched. He could still feel the sharp points of pain around his wings and turned his pain receptors down almost as far as he could. He didn't want to turn them all the way off, because then he might not notice if he sustained even greater damage to his body. Rather than immediately moving, he held still and did what Tristan referred to as "gathering his wits together" and "took stock" of his situation. (Harry spared a moment to appreciate that Tristan's aphorisms were turning out to be so applicable to this situation, just as Tristan's plumbing words had come in handy when Elena's phone got killed.) He focused on recalling the last thing he could remember: watching the fuzzy white ball arc into his sitting area. He remembered the odd smell, and realized he must have been drugged and kidnapped, but who would do such a thing?

Ah. Could it be that Critter finally went "off the deep end"? It seemed far-fetched, but Critter's comments on Harry's posted photo had become somewhat more intense lately. Harry hadn't been concerned because Tristan and Elena hadn't been concerned, but he felt he might have to change his position on that issue. For now, though, he decided he first needed to somehow get himself decoupled from the surface onto which he was stuck. When he recalled what he had been through recently with the devouring drain, his current circumstances just didn't seem that catastrophic comparatively speaking. His thinking had cleared up nicely, but his wings were damaged and his arms and legs were very stiff. Despite his physical condition, Harry was confident he would be able to achieve his goal of unstuck freedom, then he would find out *WTF* was going on here. He had to free at least one wing so that he could move enough to see his surroundings.

Harry tried lifting his right wing. He felt a significant twinge of pain, even with the pain receptors nearly all the way off, which really annoyed him. He tried lifting the wing again, and this time "added some sauce" to his effort. Having put that bit of extra oomph into his movement, Harry felt his right wing pop free at the same time he heard a sharp *ping*, followed by a glimpse of something long, thin, and metallic flying over his head. He couldn't lift his wing farther, but he had achieved enough mobility on that side that he could lift his head slightly, enough to reconnoiter the immediate area on his right before taking further action. Harry wasn't one to blindly race down the dark basement stairs, calling out "who's there?" after hearing a suspicious noise coming from below; he knew that was a bad idea. In this situation, he had no intention of becoming a casualty of his own stupidity.

Keeping his movements small and slow, he looked around as much as he could. He could see that he seemed to be hanging from a smallish corkboard, which in turn was hanging on a wall in the dark room. Turning his head to the left, he saw that his left wing was literally pinned down— there was a long, silvery straight pin poked through his wing and into the board. He was incredulous, then furious; some bastard had mounted an insect display, with Harry as the focal point. Disregarding the pain, he forcibly twisted and lifted his left wing, jostling the pin loose, to send it aloft and away.

With both wings now released, Harry fell a long way down, landing on the carpeted floor directly under the corkboard. He tried to soften the landing by fluttering his wings on the way down, but the pinholes, together with his general bodily stiffness, made maneuvering difficult. He could see his aquarium sitting on a small desk at the far side of the room, but as the aquarium was made of clear glass it didn't make for much of a hiding place. Harry spied a floor vent nearby; it seemed there was always a floor vent somewhere when he needed it. He limped across the carpet, dragging his wings behind him, and stuffed himself between the vent's vanes, down into a dark, dusty conduit that ran laterally beneath the flooring. Wanting to be sure he couldn't be reached, he forced himself to traverse the conduit for several yards farther before he felt safer. He sank down, exhaustion finally overcoming him. Before he let himself sleep, he engaged a small energy shield to deter the types of other beings that might bother him in this place. He hadn't felt the need for a shield for a long time and it wouldn't deter the much larger being who had stolen him, but he'd deal with that one when he woke.

Harry was awakened several hours later by the sound of a door opening in the room above him. He had been able to sleep long enough to mostly heal the puncture holes in his wings and reduce his general stiffness a little. He was hungry and thirsty but remained still and alert, listening for other sounds coming from above. He heard what seemed to be the ruffle of pages, followed by a thud of something hitting the floor, perhaps a notebook flung aside, then rapid footsteps moving across the room to where the corkboard still hung. There was a gasp and a high-pitched distressed cry, then rapid footsteps going to the other side of the room where Harry had seen his aquarium placed. There was a quieter thump, accompanied by soft moans. Harry assumed his kidnapper had dropped to the floor and now sounded distressed. Harry smiled smugly and began a careful grooming. Food and water could wait a bit longer. He had to figure out how to exit the conduit, get outside, and get back to Tristan and Elena, all without being recaptured. He would hate to leave his aquarium and phone behind, but it couldn't be helped. He began musing how to accomplish his escape, first giving some very warm thought to revenge:

Serves you right, you bastard! Pin an innocent being to a board, will you? I need to come up some special kind of "just desserts," especially for you.

The moaning stopped abruptly. "Wh-what was that? Is someone there?"

Harry stopped in mid-groom, one hand poised over his head. He had not voiced his thought, he was sure of that, nor had he projected it, but somehow the thieving bastard, presumably Critter, had "heard" him. *Huh.* This situation now held great potential for Harry's entertainment. He had gotten so used to being able to speak aloud that he had put this other form of communication to the side. The "shouting into someone's brain" form took a bit more energy, true, but he was feeling pretty strong at the moment. He threw out another thought, in a purposely spooky tone:

It's your conscience, you—you assassin!

Harry waited for a reaction and was pleased to hear frantic scrambling footsteps race across the room, then the door banged shut and quiet returned. He extended his awareness and could sense that Critter had not only fled the room, they apparently had also exited the building. Based on the kidnapper's fading, attenuated thoughts that Harry could still discern, they were proceeding rapidly down the street in front of the dwelling where they had stashed him, their victim. It was Harry's opportunity for escape, but he needed to let his family know he was okay first. They were probably worried sick. What to do, what to do...

Harry's wings were functional; truth be told, he felt pretty good. He recalled that he had a phone stuck to one end of his aquarium, and that his aquarium was accessible now that Critter had run off. He decided to go back into the room above and figure out how to use his phone to message his family before Critter returned. After that, he thought he could probably crawl through the gap under the door and eventually escape the building. Or, if Critter returned first, Harry planned to fly through the open door before Critter could grab him again. And, Harry thought grimly, if Critter did happen to capture him again, Critter was quite literally in for the shock of their life.

When he got back to his aquarium, Harry checked the

remaining battery life on his phone and saw that it was under fifty percent. The charger cord was still connected to the phone at one end and the charging block at the other end. Unfortunately, it had all been tossed into the aquarium and lay there in a disorganized pile. Harry didn't want to take the time to fool with this, but he thought that he might need the phone again at some point. He paced over to the block and stood contemplating it. He knew from past experience that such blocks were heavy, at least to him. However, this block looked much smaller than the one he had struggled with only a few days ago. Must be newer tech. He decided to "give it a go" and thought about how to lift it. The cord and block were new, having come with the phone; he tested the connections and found that both were snug and unlikely to drop off. He could see a conveniently placed wall outlet behind the desk on which the aquarium had been placed. He decided the best approach was to grasp the cord where it connected to the block and airlift the block out of the aquarium.

The smaller block weighed significantly less than he had anticipated, and Harry was able to easily lift it up and out of the aquarium. He dropped it behind the desk and followed it down to where it lay under the outlet. Harry had never tried plugging anything into an outlet, but how hard could it be? He couldn't see any immediate danger, but unseen dangers were usually the worst kind. He didn't have other options, so he picked up the block again and flitted his wings so that he slowly rose to the level of the outlet. He aligned the two prongs on the block with the outlet aperture, then firmly pushed the block forward. Harry had to give the block another especially hard push in order to get it properly seated in the outlet. Remaining aloft, he backed up and reviewed his work. The connection looked good to him. He buzzed back up to the desk and dropped into the aquarium. He powered up the phone and saw that it was indeed charging. He opened the messaging app and happened to find the speech-to-text mode, and hurriedly dictated a brief message to his family. He was satisfied it would hold them out of panic until he could get back home, since it wasn't like they could call 911 for help.

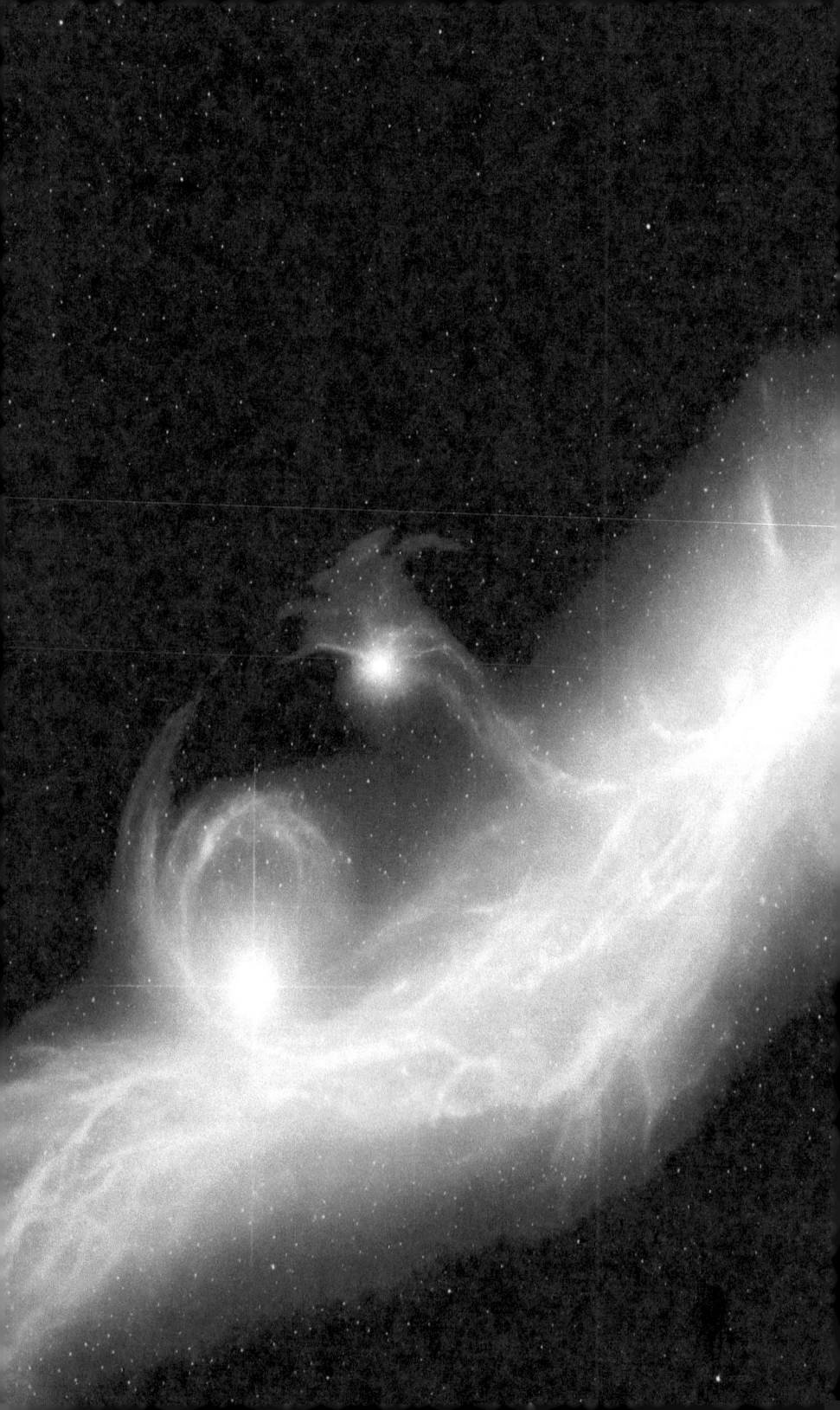

CHAPTER THREE

I call 911 for help as soon as we realize Harry's been kidnapped. As it's early Sunday morning and not a Friday or Saturday night, a patrol car quickly arrives. We had explained to the officers that our home had been broken into and that a rare, highly valuable pet had been kidnapped, er, stolen, although I stumble a bit on describing Harry as a pet. The high-value-pet theft interests the officers, until we show them Harry's photo for identification, and their eyebrows pretty much disappear up under their hat brims. One of them mutters something along the lines of "*What the hell, this is a bug!*" When Elena hears that, she starts crying again and the officer at least looks embarrassed. They are clearly perplexed by all the emotion directed towards a "bug." We explain how Elena found Harry and that he appears to be an unknown species we hope to have formally classified at some point. Not exactly the whole truth, since obviously I can't explain Harry himself. I don't want to be the guy who gets arrested for acting crazy— you know, like the methed-out "Florida Man" riding a gator down the street.

We aren't able to provide an approximate value, other than our opinion of "our pet" being priceless, but the officers write in their notebooks "sentimental value." I direct the officers' attention to Critter; unfortunately, they don't think Critter's posted comments are particularly threatening. Free speech strikes again. The officers are sympathetic, of course, but are also candid, saying this appears to be a minor break-in and there have been no other reports of burglaries in the immediate neighborhood. They think it was more likely kids breaking in on a dare, which apparently has happened recently in other parts of town. They say the pet theft was one of convenience: wrong time, wrong place for Harry. The officers agree to look into it, but it's clear to us they think it's unlikely they'll apprehend anyone, let alone get Harry back. They recommend I install a camera monitoring system, which isn't a bad idea, but Elena and I are certain we already know what happened.

We wrap up things with the officers and I escort them out. My thoughts are a jumbled mess that provide no comfort as I go back into the living room to rejoin Elena, who is still sitting on the couch, clutching a box of tissues. I sit down beside her and take her chilled hand in mine. She's stopped crying for the most part, but we are both still massively upset. She blames herself, but of course I say that's nonsense. If anything, it's my fault for failing to protect us. She blots her eyes again and takes a deep breath.

"Tristan, what are we going to do? We have to go get him, but we have no idea where to even start looking."

I don't have an answer, or even a man-plan at this point, since I'm still processing the situation myself. My phone buzzes in my pocket as a new text message comes in. I'm inclined to ignore it, but then I have the crazy thought it might be a ransom demand. I can feel my temper rising and struggle to grab the phone with a shaking hand. I open the text and jump to my feet with a shout, badly startling Elena. "Tristan, what is it? They haven't killed him, have they?" "He's okay, he's okay! He sent us a text, that clever

little bug!"

"He's not actually a—"

I impatiently wave that away and read Harry's text aloud: *"Hi family, this is Harry. You've probably noticed by now that I've been stolen, but I'm absolutely okay, so no worries there. My kidnapper has fled the premises and I will be leaving shortly myself. It will take me some time to get back but I will get back, never fear! In the meantime, use your patience and relax, I'll be fine. Gotta go now."*

We have mirroring stunned looks on our faces. This is an incredible switch-up in a situation that we think is still pretty dicey, in spite of Harry's apparent bravado. My knees feel weak all of a sudden and I drop down onto the couch beside Elena. I hold my phone up so that we can re-read Harry's message together. We do that several times before I feel I can put the phone down. I'm very careful to not delete the text as I close the messaging app. I think through the steps Harry would have had to take in order to get his text out—it's a long message for someone who can't type.

"I'm pretty impressed with Harry. I know he's resourceful, he has to be, but this is way beyond anything I would have thought he was capable of." I have a sudden thought and snap my fingers with excitement. "He must have used the speech-to-text mode to do this! How f...ah—effing smart is that? Hey! Did you ever download that 'Find My Phone' app?"

Elena blots her eyes again and I get to see her luminous smile. "That is definitely pretty smart, and I absolutely effing did download that app."

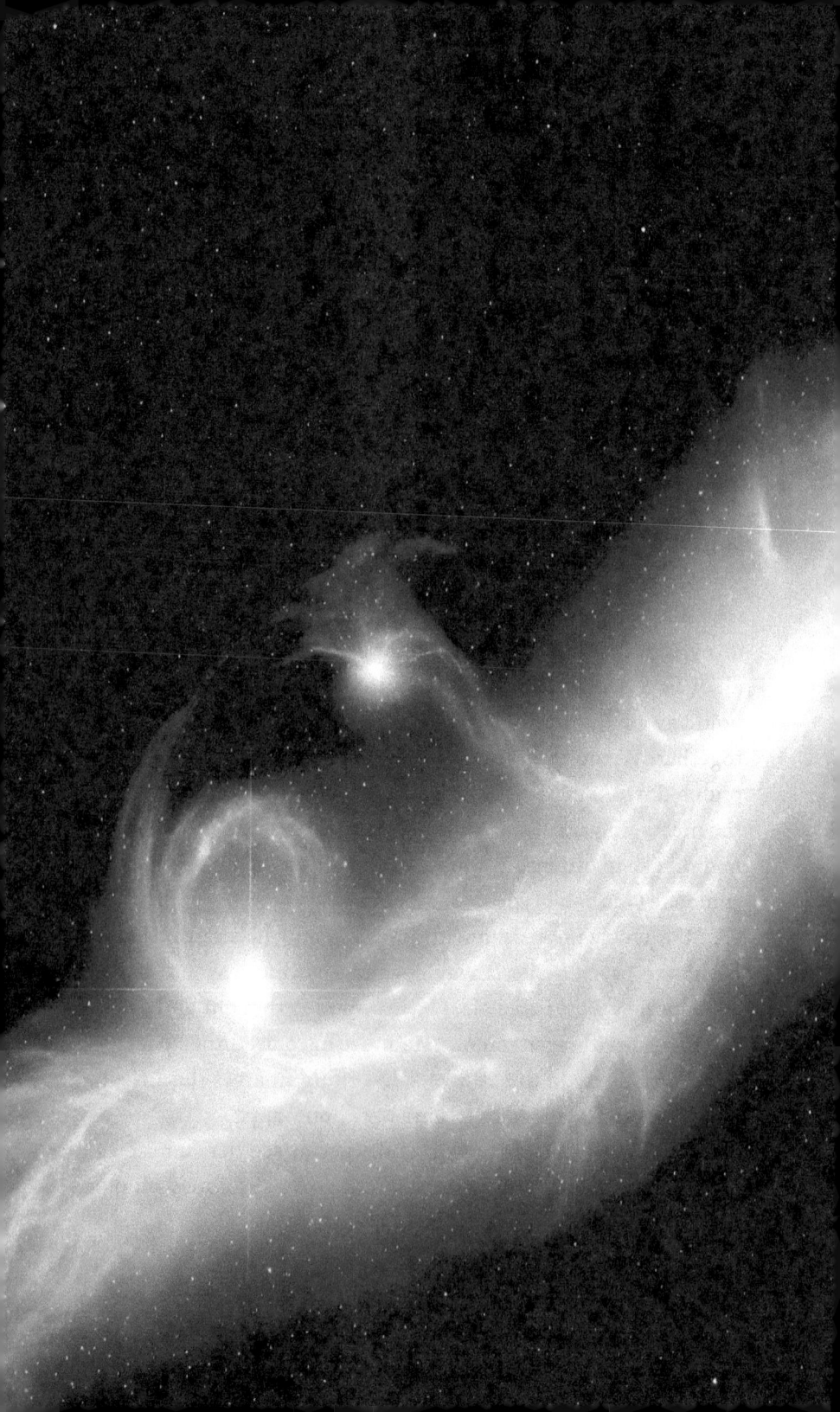

CHAPTER FOUR

Just as he hit the 'send' icon, Harry heard footsteps approaching the closed door. He quickly flew out of the aquarium to the other side of the room, dove back through the vent, and quietly moved far enough down the conduit to be out of reach of a standard-length human arm. Then he moved a little farther, just in case. He hoped Critter wouldn't notice the charger had been plugged in, but even if they did it wouldn't make a difference to Harry's current plans. He was determined he was going home and Critter would interfere only at their peril. The footsteps stopped outside the door; after a moment or so Harry could hear the very faint sweeping noise of the door being slowly opened across the carpet. There were two steps into the room, a pause, then two more steps. He heard the door close quietly. Consciously not projecting his words, he thought *"what now?"* and felt the tiniest bit of anxiety.

A curious miasma of all-consuming, frightened and desolate emotions coming from Critter pushed its way into Harry's mind. He heard a small thump overhead, as if someone had suddenly sat down on the floor. He thought this was odd; he had expected to have to wait through a certain amount of storming about, ranting and raving, on Critter's part. Instead, he heard them cough and clear their throat, then a tense, thin jittery voice was audible:

"I'm not sure if I'm hallucinating now or if something is actually here. In case this isn't a hallucination, let me just say that I may have made a couple of bad choices lately. If I had known for sure you were an alien, I wouldn't have treated you like a regular insect. I mean, I always *thought* you were probably an alien."

That statement had a lot to unpack overall, but Critter didn't sound nearly repentant enough to suit Harry. He was outraged and didn't bother to keep his thoughts to himself.

"Bad choices? Are you serious right now? You stole me and did your best to kill me! That goes well beyond simple bad choices. And just for the record, I'm not an alien. Why in the name of all that's holy do I have to keep having this discussion!"

Harry hadn't meant to shout, but there had been an emphatic, powerful outward thrust in his last thought-statement to his kidnapper. In response there came a loud thumping sound, as if Critter had bumped into a chair and sent it crashing over to lie on the floor. He heard Critter pacing around the room, the sound of their footsteps muffled by the many layers of building materials between them and Harry—carpet, padding, plywood flooring, wiring, and more. The despair emanating from Critter grew so intense that Harry thought he could almost see the dense, dark energy it was creating. Harry wondered anxiously if he might have agitated things a couple of steps too far. How far could one push a crazy person before that person started acting even more crazy, possibly tipping over into homicide? Harry had the manic thought that in his case homicide wasn't the correct term—perhaps insecticide?

The alien part of Harry's declamation was admittedly disingenuous of him, since he actually didn't know for a fact he wasn't an alien—he had simply decided he wasn't and run with it. He may have voicelessly screamed a little in frustration. Harry wished he had thought to throw in some plumbing words for emphasis, but he figured the conversation wasn't over yet so there was still time for that.

"Okay, okay, but I mean, realistically, I don't know what else you could be *but* an alien. I'll have to take your word for it that you're not."

Harry ground his teeth and clenched his mittens. This was too much, just too much. He had been grievously injured and was mightily offended. He knew it was bad form, but he really wanted to, to—taser, yeah—this Critter until their hair smoked. Harry took several deep, calming breaths and stopped to consider there was more than a good chance Critter was a psychopath. Based on his having been drugged, kidnapped, and stabbed with pins, Harry already knew Critter was inherently dangerous. He had seen TV shows about this kind of thing, which rarely ended well for the victim. As well, the depth and intensity of that emotional wave he had felt was very concerning. Harry wondered how Critter was able to think, let alone converse, considering the thick fog of despair and fear that enveloped them.

Harry would have to be extremely cautious and wait for Critter to leave before exiting the conduit again. He was feeling hunger pangs and wondered how long he'd have to wait before he could find food and water. He refused to dwell on that. Critter cleared their throat again and from the shuffling sounds Harry could hear above his head, they were slowly moving around the room. Harry thought that Critter was probably trying to find his hiding place and was glad this so-called "telepathy" couldn't be traced directionally. At least he wouldn't give away his own position. His attention was called back when Critter started speaking again:

"What if I agree to take you back to your home, unharmed, er—I mean with no *further* harm—if you'll stay here just a little while longer so we can talk some more. More than ever, I *need* to know what you are. I *need* to understand whether this event is just another form of my hallucinations. Listen, so that you can think about that without having to worry about me being here, I'll go out of the house for a while."

Harry heard a louder rustle of movement and then the door opening and closing, taking away Critter's dark aura as well. He leaned back against the curvature of the conduit and let himself relax. He had been very tense throughout that exchange and his muscles ached; maybe he wasn't fully recovered after all. He had no way of knowing whether his captor might be able to find his hiding place and worried over that for a few minutes. He didn't believe Critter would keep their bargain. Harry couldn't risk it and decided to stay with his own plan, which seemed to be validated when the door opened and Harry heard Critter return to the room above.

"Before I go, I brought some food and water for you. Just in case you're not actually a hallucination. I'm going to put it on the desk beside that aquarium. I'll be back in a couple of hours, and I hope we can talk. I'm very sorry I hurt you."

Harry heard Critter leave the room again and go down some stairs that seemed to be at the end of a short hallway from the room he was in. Another door slammed shut farther away, sounding lower and toward the front of the building. Harry was relieved Critter had mentioned leaving the "house," as he had assumed he was most likely in a mad scientist's lair in an abandoned warehouse somewhere. This room seemed to be on an upper floor, which could cause some complications for his plans. He had thought the layout would be more like his family's house—all on one level with relatively easy access to the outdoors. It didn't matter; he was a flyer now, no need to worry about walking distances, regardless of the number of legs he had. Harry waited until the house was absolutely still, then looked through the vent into the room, in case Critter had silently re-entered, or hadn't left at all. However, the room appeared to be empty of humans, or other types of living beings for that matter. The other beings still pinned to the corkboard didn't venture an opinion on the situation.

After the police leave, we relocate to the kitchen. Elena sits at the table and brings up the 'Find My Phone' app while I put on a pot of coffee. We're going to need the caffeine and I intend to go hog wild with the sugar. It's still pretty early and we haven't eaten yet, so I throw a couple bagels in the toaster. Elena has already added Harry's phone to the app by then and is going through the steps to find it when I sit beside her to watch. Finally, a map comes up with an arrow pointing to a location just as the toaster pops up the bagels. The coffee has dripped enough to give us about a half cup of coffee each to start with. We tear into bagels and coffee while Elena manipulates the map to enlarge the pinpointed location and we start making our plan.

I look at the address and realize it's actually not that far from our house, maybe thirty minutes or so. I enter the location into the GPS app on my phone. Elena is anxious to leave right damn now; she jumps up from the table and power-walks into the living room. She grabs her purse from the couch and starts looking for her car keys, but I think we need to do some actual planning first.

"Elena, let's just stop for a minute and figure this out. We think the person who took Harry is probably Critter, but we don't know that. It might really have been kids. We can't go off with no idea what we're going to do when we get there. We can't just go up and ring the bell and say give us back our bug."

She sits back down on the couch, holding her purse and jacket on her lap and a fierce, stubborn look on her face. "I think that's exactly what we should do. I don't know why we can't do that."

I scrub my beard-prickly face with my hands and sit in the recliner. "I want to see what kind of place he's stashed in first. The place has everything to do with what we might be able to do to get him back."

She tosses her purse and jacket aside and jumps up, reaching for my phone. I kind of duck and hand it to her at the same time.

"I'll bet Google Earth can show us what kind of place is at that location." She taps furiously for a few seconds, then triumphantly shows me the display screen.

"Look, it's a house, a two-story house. What did you expect, a mad scientist's lair in an abandoned warehouse somewhere? Can we go now? What do we need to take with us? Flashlights? Rope? Duct tape? I have makeup we can use to put that black stripe under our eyes. Come on, get up, we have a lot to do."

I'm so surprised that I also jump up; we end up standing almost toe-to-toe. "First of all, I *guarantee* we will not be doing this at night, so flashlights are not needed. Football players put that black stuff under their eyes, not kidnappers, which is what we'll look like if we show up with rope and duct tape. It's the middle of Sunday morning and it's not like people will all be at work, so, *witnesses*. What exactly are you planning to do? We are not, I repeat not, a SWAT team!"

Her eyes look like they're hot and shiny, almost like she has a fever. I've never seen her like this before, but then we've never had a loved one kidnapped before, either. She emphatically stabs a forefinger at my chest and I reactively take a step back.

"Okay, Mr. Super Cautious, here's what I'm planning to do. I'm *planning* to go there whether it's night or day, and I am taking a flashlight, which incidentally makes a pretty good cudgel if you use it correctly. After I use the flashlight, I'm *planning* on tying someone up until the police can come get them while we run away with Harry. I'm *planning* to bring him home. Do you really think the police are going to help us get Harry back? He doesn't mean anything to them!"

I narrow my eyes suspiciously at her. "How do you know about 'correctly' using a flashlight as a cudgel?"

"Self-defense training, how else? TV shows? Hah, those don't show you how to swing it so it connects right. You want to knock out, not kill. Well, mostly not kill, obviously it depends on the situation. Whatever, let's not waste more time arguing. Just get whatever you think you'll need and meet me at my car, it's less conspicuous than your truck."

With that, she turns and hurries out to the backyard shed, where unfortunately we do have both rope and duct tape. I'm dumbfounded, but I do as I'm told and go to find myself a flashlight.

Harry slowly and cautiously began climbing up the conduit to the vent, stopping every few seconds to reassess the seeming emptiness of the room. He sat near the vent for a time, peering through the slots to get his bearings. He could see the two small dishes sitting on the desk but was reluctant to move away from his hiding place. Finally, he decided he had to take the chance and squeezed through a slot again, then quickly flitted from the floor to the desktop. Before he drank any water, he paused to let his senses determine if there was anything non-water in the water, but it seemed to be fresh and clear. He kept an eye on the door while he took a long drink. He felt as if the drug Critter used on him had dried out all his tissues and thought he could feel them expanding as he drank. After his drink, he examined the contents of the other small dish. He was unfamiliar with the type of food it held, but it didn't set off any sensory alarms for potential harm. The food was some sort of dried, crumbly material. He broke off a small piece and brought it up to his face in order to examine it more closely, then lurched back in horror when he realized that the material was dried crickets. Harry was a vegetarian, having tested that idea against an ant when he first came out his most recent stasis. It had been a novel experience to feel the gag reflex in his new throat.

Harry was very hungry by now, not having had any food for what seemed like at least two days. Even so, he didn't feel he'd be able to choke down dried, dusty crickets, let alone keep them down. He sat despondently beside the dish, looking around the room to see if there were any other options, any at all. He saw there was a cluttered worktable butted up against the room's other wall, situated directly above the floor vent. Harry saw cotton balls, forceps, bottles—the implements of his near-demise—lying about on the tabletop, which made him feel angry and upset again as he flew up to sit on the table's outside edge. He distractedly glanced over the littered tabletop and caught a glimpse of what appeared to be a food wrapper. Thinking there might be something still in the wrapper, some crumbs maybe, he flitted over to investigate. The wrapper lay underneath a few loose pieces of paper, almost out of sight. Harry pushed the papers to the side so he could see the wrapper more clearly. The wrapper turned out to be an opened packet, with labeling that read "Chocolate Covered Espresso Beans." The packet still contained a number of roundish items that Harry assumed were the beans mentioned on the label. Harry knew about coffee beans and had heard the term "espresso," but he wasn't sure what, if any, relationship there might be between the two.

However, he considered that: 1), chocolate, in his experience, was very good to eat and not harmful at all; and 2), beans of any sort were definitely not crickets. He couldn't see a downside and pulled a few of the beans out of the packet. A couple got loose and rolled off the table onto the floor, out of sight, but there still remained plenty for Harry's needs. He began munching away and found that he really loved those beans, and quickly finished off three before he felt full. Harry thought the beans were so good that he should stash a few in his aquarium. Having decided that, Harry grabbed a bean with both mittens and flitted across the room. He landed in front of the phone and placed the bean on the floor underneath it, up against the glass wall upon which the phone was mounted. He was starting to feel pretty energetic. His wings were almost buzzing on their own, and his pulse was ramping up.

Harry felt like he could move the moon; moving the little beans was no effort at all! It took him only a few minutes to get the rest of the beans lined up under the phone. He counted six in all that were left after the three he had already eaten. He thought he should probably have some sort of little cupboard in which he could keep his movie snacks and started flitting around the room looking for building materials. He felt power-ful, like nothing was beyond him, that it would take him no effort at all to build a cupboard. He was sure he'd have it finished well before Critter would be back. It occurred to him that he could also use a coffee table, and maybe a bookcase. The possibilities were endless, hampered only by obtaining access to the right materials. And tools—he'd probably need a few tools that would fit his mittens. He'd have to improvise, of course, as always.

He flew in circles around the room with increasing speed, scouting the territory but not finding anything useful in the way of either materials or tools. His aerial recon began to slow down, and things were looking blurry due to his quivering eyeballs. He was feeling a little off, like he wasn't getting enough air. His could feel his pulse pounding in his ears and there was definitely a headache starting behind his eyes. His ears were throbbing in time with his pulse. He was puzzled by all this, because he still felt powerful and wanted to get started on his building projects. Suddenly he felt faint, and quickly headed for his aquarium in case he needed to lie down. He landed near his phone and was surprised to feel that his wings were still buzzing, even though he wasn't flying. He forcefully folded them under the wing covers along his sides. His knees trembled and sweat beaded his forehead as he staggered to his sitting area. He felt really ill and thought maybe the beans weren't that good for him after all. He sadly thought his projects would have to be put on hold until he felt better and closed his shivering eyelids for just a minute to rest his eyes.

Harry had a chance to have a short rest before he was awakened by the sound of the door opening in the lower part of the house. He was still a little shaky, but quickly flew out of the aquarium and back to the vent, listening as slow footsteps trudged up the apparently uncarpeted stairs and down the hall, stopping outside the door. Before the doorknob turned Harry was comfortably back in his hideout. Harry felt the aura of abject defeat and despair precede Critter into the room. There was a soft thump above his head; presumably, Critter was now sitting on the floor. Harry wondered if he should make the first comment, but Critter started speaking first, in a soft, tightly controlled voice.

"Maybe you could come out so we can introduce ourselves?"

A memory of Saint James, the monastery cat from so long ago, issuing a similar invitation flashed through Harry's mind and he laughed out loud. He wasn't going to fall for that again.

"I'm not coming out, because I'm not an idiot. You need to get out of here and leave me alone before I call 911."

Harry felt Critter's jolt of surprise and cursed himself for possibly giving away the phone being charged. Maybe Critter had been so focused on Harry that they hadn't even noticed the phone. He didn't hear further movement from above, though, so perhaps the phone was safe. He heard Critter sigh deeply.

"I know you have no reason at all to trust me. I don't know how to fix that."

The utter defeat in Critter's voice was real, and Harry could feel it embedded in the dark aura emanating from them. He realized that he might not have as much to fear from Critter now as he obviously had earlier in their relationship. Somewhat against his better judgement, Harry thought he might be able to meet his nemesis halfway. He'd fly up to a high point in the room and be ready to escape when an opportunity arose.

"Tell you what. I'll come out now, but I still don't feel safe around you. If you agree to move your chair over by the door and to stay on your chair, I'll come out."

"No problem, I'll stay over there and give you a lot of space. Okay, I'm settled in. You can come out now."

PART THREE
PRESENT DAY

S ilence descended from above. Harry took a deep breath and slowly walked to the end of the conduit. He peeked out from below the vent before going farther, but his sightline was such that all he could see of Critter was the toe of a tattered sneaker, jerkily tapping on the carpet. The toe of the shoe was way over by the door, so he squeezed himself up through the vent, into the room once more. He sat on the vent for a moment to make sure Critter wasn't sneaking back over by the desk. He risked looking around the leg of the worktable and saw that Critter was indeed settled on their chair, on the other side of the room, with their feet tucked behind the front chair legs and their hands tightly clenched between their knees. There was enough space between them that Harry was confident Critter wouldn't be able to jump up and grab him before he could fly to safety. He couldn't see any form of capture implement— spray, net, whatever—in Critter's hands or near them. Harry took two steps farther from the vent, which put him in full view of his captor.

Critter gasped and watched him with wide eyes and

dropped jaw but didn't move from their chair. Harry noticed that while the room itself was generally organized and tidy, the person sitting against the door was much less so. They wore denim jeans cut off above the knee, a discolored tee- shirt, and dirty sneakers with no socks. Despite their dusky skin tone, their arms and legs showed several dark bruises, which Harry assumed had been obtained during the raid on his home. Their hair was in massive disarray, with curls spiking out in all directions. Their clothes were wrinkled, and there was a faint, unappealing odor about them.

Harry was by no means an expert on human gender designations, but this untidy small person sure looked female to him, and a relatively young one at that. He was startled to realize he had assumed all along that he'd been kidnapped by a man, most likely a man younger than Tristan, but definitely a man in his mind. Not that it made a difference, captured was captured, but this made Harry think he needed to work on his unconscious gender biases.

Critter made a sort of choking sound, as if she was having trouble putting her thoughts into words but couldn't actually voice them.

"Since we're being so friendly and all, I'd like to try talking aloud with you. Is that something you think you can handle? What is your name?"

"I guess—I guess I can manage it. My name is Bakari. It's an African name that means 'promising.'" I haven't exactly lived up to it, at least not yet. I know your name is Harry."

Harry was sorely tempted to keep calling her "Assassin," but he decided he had bigger issues to fry.

"I assume you got my name from the Instagram post. Next time I'll make sure to know what someone intends to do with their photo of me."

Bakari's eyelids flickered, and although she swayed a little, she managed to stay upright on the chair pushed against the door. She moistened her lips and managed to get a disbelieving whisper out that Harry could barely hear.

"You can *actually* talk." She shrank back in her chair and spoke as if talking to herself. "I'd think I'm having an auditory hallucination on top of a visual one, but my hallucinations don't normally have conversations with me. So maybe my condition has turned even worse. There's a happy thought." She shook her head fiercely and refocused on Harry. "Just to check, you're a praying mantis, and they don't bite, right?"

Harry extended his wings and flitted up to sit on the desktop, outside his aquarium. He regarded Bakari and thought with interest that he hadn't known a human's eyes could open that wide. He sat back, as well as he could, and crossed his arms.

"Yes, I'm presently configured as something that looks like a praying mantis. Non-biting, and not a hallucination. I'm not actually a mantis, of course, as you've most likely realized by now. I have actual bones and organs and everything, on the inside. I'd like to leave here very soon, intact if you please, but I'll be courteous—more courteous than you have been—and give you a few minutes to talk."

Bakari looked down at her feet and spoke in a low voice. "I'm pretty sure the talking is the hallucination part. Anyway, I know there's no excuse for my actions toward you, but there is a reason, more an explanation, really, if you'd care to hear it."

Harry remained offended. "I'm not sure I would ever agree there could be such a reason, but I will listen to what you have to say."

"I did get your name from that post, but that's all there was to gain from that posting. Since your owners wouldn't help me, I had to do research on my own. But I could never come up with anything that matched you and I guess now I know why. I thought the only way to learn about you was to obtain you for more, ah—direct—study."

Harry snorted and shook his head. "So to you, *'direct study'* means murder? It seems to me there were a few other options that could have been used. Like, oh, I don't know, create better Internet search parameters or something. Options not harmful to living beings, whether they can communicate or not."

He was nearly ranting now. "And by the way, I don't have 'owners.' I have a *family*. You took me away from my *family*. You've hurt more than just me. You do know that your posts had the ring of crazy to them, right? *Of course* they were ignored. I'm waiting to hear your justifications for your criminal behavior, and never forget that it was, in fact, criminal."

He was gratified to see her wince and squirm, looking anywhere but directly at him.

"I agree, okay? It was criminal behavior. I'm very thankful I didn't kill you completely. I sure thought I had. Let me tell you my story, and maybe there will be some way you can forgive me. Maybe you can think of some sort of penance I could do that would make it up to you. Can you hear me out?"

Harry wasn't inclined in any way to be trusting but he was also pretty curious, which he knew was not necessarily one of his more objective modes. He thought he was safe for the moment, since he could jump back down the vent before Bakari could get across the room. It occurred to him that while *technically* he couldn't bite, he could pretend to bite while administering a good static zap without having to use much energy. He folded his arms across his chest with a *humph*. He was still very angry, and the biting idea seemed attractive.

"Fine. I have some questions first. How old are you, anyway? Where is *your* family?"

H arry could hear Bakari's harsh, stressed breathing and mentally kicked himself for automatically feeling guilty; *he* wasn't the villain here. Even so, he thought he should try to make things a little less emotionally fraught if he wanted to exit this place in one, preferably living, piece.

"Listen, I think we both need to take a breath and regroup. To recap: I am anxious to be gone from here. You appear reluctant to let me go until I've heard your story. Very well. I will listen to your story, provided that when your story is finished you will leave this room, leaving the door open behind you. You will then leave this building, also leaving the front door open. I will leave under my own power and find my own way home."

The harsh breathing slowed, to Harry's relief, but the aura of sorrow and despair lingered. Harry set that complication aside for the moment. There was a long pause, and Harry waited uneasily for an agreement to his proposal. After a few moments, Bakari began speaking again, in a rattled, raspy voice.

"I agree to your plan. I will try to calm down." Bakari drew her feet up and awkwardly sat cross-legged on the chair. She was still suspecting hallucinations, but at least she could have a conversation. She absently twisted an errant curl, then tucked it behind her ear, and moistened her dry lips.

"Um. I'm almost seventeen, and..."

Harry didn't know everything about humans, but he knew that "almost seventeen" meant sixteen years old, possibly even just barely turned sixteen. This was indeed a young person, who should certainly still have been under some sort of parental or other adult supervision. He had a few suspicions.

"You snuck out, didn't you? Where are your parents?"

Bakari scowled defiantly and crossed her arms over her chest. "If you must know, they're out of town at a business meeting. My aunt was here, but she had to leave for an emergency of some kind with my cousin. I was supposed to go to my uncle's, but I told him my aunt would be back soon."

Harry did a face-palm. "I can't believe this. You're a delinquent!"

She unfolded her arms impatiently and swung her feet back to the floor but stayed put on her chair. "Look, you don't understand." She shook her head, talking to herself in a low voice. "How could you, since you're a hallucination?"

"I've told you, I'm not a hallucination. Explain yourself!"

"Fine! Give me a minute, will you? This isn't exactly easy, you know. You're either a visual and auditory hallucination, which is very probable, or you're an alien. Since you vigorously denied being an alien, that leaves the hallucination option, since I *know* there aren't talking bugs on Earth."

Harry threw his arms wide in frustration. "And you know everything on Earth there is to know, right? Nothing slips by you, I guess. Fine, let's go with the hallucination then, whatever will get this over with. I want to get out of here."

Bakari slumped down, her momentary spark of defiance flickering out. Still not looking directly at Harry, she twisted her fingers together until her knuckles paled. She took a deep breath, let it out, and began speaking in a quiet, tremulous voice.

"I'm not a delinquent. I've never done anything like this before. I have a—medical condition—that I manage less effectively at times. When my condition gets bad, it helps me to focus on something so exclusively that everything else fades away. Unfortunately, sometimes that exclusive focus becomes obsession.

"As early as I can remember, I could see things that others couldn't. To me it was like there was a movie, or TV show, running in the back of my mind. Low visibility—like watching a street scene through heavy fog. When I was real little I tried to get my parents to 'watch the show' with me. They thought I had imaginary friends, a phase that would pass in time. Sometimes they'd pretend they could see them, try to play with them and me. I remember thinking how silly they looked doing that. I was probably around five when I finally understood that no one else could see what I did, so I quit talking about it.

"As I got older, I started becoming more deeply involved with the images; well, not images exactly, but whole scenes being played out. This wasn't happening in the background any longer. The more attention I paid to the scenes, the clearer they became. I didn't understand any of them, and some were pretty freaking scary. My attention was totally absorbed while I watched, to the extent I was nearly non-responsive to other interactions until whatever scene I was watching ended. This worried my parents far more than what they had thought were imaginary friends, but the doctors said I'd grow out of it."

Harry was feeling restive and not inclined to be patient with this rambling story. Bakari had certainly scared *him*. Harry could hear the chair creak again and saw her shifting a little to become more comfortable. He almost wished he could stick pins in her to see how she liked it; perhaps that would move this situation along to the point where Harry was finally freed. He decided to agitate the conversation more speedily toward his goal.

He buzzed his wings briefly in irritation. "This is all very interesting, but what does it have to do with you kidnapping me? I don't see the connection. You can forget about trying to make me feel sympathy for your so-called suffering, much less becoming attached to you. *This* prisoner won't be developing Stockholm syndrome, I can tell you that much right now."

Bakari paused, not sure how to proceed. "I have to provide the background so that what I struggle with *now* makes sense. I'm not trying for your sympathy, but I hope I can get your understanding. I don't know whether you'll ever forgive me. I just want to try to make you understand how I got to this point."

Harry wasn't inclined to be forgiving. "This will never make sense to me. You actually *are* delusional if you think you can ever make me understand why you tried to destroy me."

Bakari inhaled a deep breath, then let it slowly hiss out, three times. She ran her hands through her hair and rubbed her face, trying to recenter herself. She took a few more deep breaths before going back to her story. Harry, being Harry, found that although he fought it, his curiosity was becoming engaged at this point. He had to remind himself that he was still extremely angry with this person. He wanted this story to be over so that he could go home, and he didn't feel particularly sympathetic to Bakari's condition. When Bakari began speaking again, her voice was marginally less strained but still tremulous.

"As I said, the closer attention I paid, the more detailed and clear the images were. By the time I was fourteen it had gotten to the point that during a hallucination, for however long it lasted I would completely stop interacting with the real world. You can imagine the effect on my family. I'll cut to the chase here and say that by the time I was fifteen I had landed in the world of serious mental health care, diagnosed with acute schizophrenia. I've read that schizophrenia is defined as '*a serious mental disorder in which people interpret reality abnormally.*' The diagnosis is based on the patient exhibiting some combination of hallucinations, delusions, and what they called 'disordered thinking.'"

Harry was a compassionate soul at the heart of his being and felt his anger toward Bakari begin to soften— slightly. He understood deep suffering. He also uncomfortably realized he might recognize some elements of Bakari's story. "So what did you do? Were the doctors able to help you?"

Bakari shuffled her feet on the floor and slumped back on the chair. After a moment, she shook her head, setting her curls bouncing. "I have a couple of opinions on that. I think the mental health team treating me is doing the best they can. Everyone is very kind and wants to help me be as well as I can be. I can't remember how many therapy sessions I've had. The doctors have tried every pharmaceutical therapy they can think of, but each medication makes my 'disordered thinking' even worse. The doctors and therapists seem to be worried that I'm going to become psychotic without the meds. They don't think I know this, but they think there's a possibility I could eventually become dangerous to others or myself."

Harry felt a little worried when he heard that. He thought Bakari actually *was* dangerous, hence the kidnapping. It seemed the connection of her mental illness to her actions against him was pretty clear. He warily watched her shift around on the chair again, still trying to get comfortable. She finally settled and continued her story.

"I act normal when I'm not hallucinating, and I don't feel ill. Well, aside from the continual stress and worry of having the hallucinations in the first place. Since the antipsychotic medications didn't end the hallucinations or make them any less intense, I stopped taking them a while ago, against doctors' orders. People were pretty unhappy about that and threatened to have me committed to long-term psychiatric care. Luckily, I've finally gotten to the point where I can communicate a little during the hallucinations, so at least people can check whether I'm on the way to a psychotic break-down. I guess that makes *them* feel better, I don't know. I do know I can't control the hallucinations or make them go away. I just have to ride them out, like a seizure. Since I'm not 'acting out,' people have relaxed a little about the meds and needing to take more extreme measures."

Harry shifted around a little himself. His muscles ached and his wings still trembled from the after-effects of the delicious beans he consumed earlier. Despite his need to remain poised for action, he let himself relax enough to take a semi-sitting position on the desktop.

"I understand you've got very serious challenges in your life, but I don't understand how that explains your actions toward me. Did you in fact have a psychotic episode? Am I still in danger from you?"

Bakari finally looked directly at Harry. He could see the immense sorrow in her expression and felt the aura of despair surrounding her become that much denser. She looked even younger than when he first saw her.

"I wasn't psychotic, I was obsessed. In the last few weeks,

the hallucinations have become more detailed than ever, and I got pretty worried. Scared, actually. I had to figure out what was real and what was imaginary. Anything outside of what I framed as my actual reality wasn't real and I could ignore it, like a movie running on the TV with the sound off. Sort of like learning to live with two different brains in the same head."

Harry was intrigued. "How were you able to tell the difference? If I understand what you're describing, the hallucinations are 'real' enough to present as reality."

Bakari snorted. "Well, I forgot to mention that I'm wicked smart. I've already completed the first three years of my online college courses. In a psychiatry major, I might add. So I can rationalize that when you know for a fact in one part of your brain that you live in a technological age, and in another part of your brain you're seeing yourself driving a carriage drawn by four horses down cobblestone streets, there are some pretty good clues there. It's more of a question of reasonableness—is it reasonable that I'd be driving a carriage and not a car? It takes serious mental effort on my part to disregard one set of images that don't make sense and act within the set that does, but I'm smart enough to manage it."

She looked away from Harry. "There are tradeoffs, though. In order to hang onto the 'real' reality, I have to obsessively focus on something so that I'm able to shut out the hallucinations. Such an intense focus quiets the part of my brain seeing something other than what I'm working on. The hallucinations have been very intense lately and I was focused on you. The obsession took over."

Bakari sighed deeply again, and Harry could see the tension increase in her neck and shoulders. "You might not believe this, but I've never broken the law before. When I saw your picture on Instagram, I had this very strong feeling that something having to do with you could help me. I actually had to sit down when it happened. I had no idea how that could be, since at the time I thought you were just a new species of insect, but I was so driven! I thought the help would come from doing such an intense study of you that I'd be able disregard the hallucinations more completely. I could immerse myself in that study and feel okay for a while. It's obvious the obsession got away from me, and I fear I might be developing that delusional thinking anyway. Maybe I *am* psychotic."

Harry winced at that—perhaps he wasn't as safe as he thought. He edged back a little, just in case. Bakari didn't seem to notice and continued speaking.

"Anyway, I thought I was managing okay. The hallucinations have gotten really brutal. Until recently they were only visual. For some reason, now I can hear things happening during the hallucination. I can nearly taste food and almost smell flowers. I'm terrified that it's possible I could start feeling pain. Some of the hallucinations have been incredibly gruesome. It's more like I'm remembering things I've experienced, but there's no way that's possible. I've just never been in the situations that I'm seeming to remember."

Uh oh. Harry thought the things Bakari had described sounded a lot like Tristan's experience when Harry mentally showed him some of Harry's memories. If Bakari was experiencing anything like that on her own, it was no wonder people think she was delusional, if not outright psychotic.

Bakari started to speak again but suddenly she shivered roughly, then seemed to freeze in place, her eyes open and glassy. Harry felt her terror wash over him; he staggered, then regained his balance. Bakari began whispering *no, no, no,* and sweat broke out on her forehead. Her shoulders twitched as if to dodge a blow and she slipped off the chair, eyes closed, to lie curled on her side on the floor. Harry could see her eyes rapidly twitching back and forth under her eyelids, as if she was watching something. Harry heard her whisper, *help me.* Tremors shook her body from head to toe, increasing in frequency and intensity as Harry watched from his spot across the room. It looked to him like something was terrifying Bakari, but there were no overt physical causes he could discern. He didn't know what to do and dithered about calling 911. He was surprised at his concern for her well-being, all things considered.

Harry was alarmed and perplexed. *What the hell is going on here?*

There could be many reasons for Bakari's reaction; even

simple dehydration could cause similarly severe symptoms. But Harry recalled Bakari's explanation of her hallucinations and paused before calling for outside help. He thought her current condition resembled a seizure, which he understood would have been caused by a misfire in her brain's communication patterns. If the problem was something like that, essentially a glitch in the matrix, perhaps it was something he could repair—unknot a tangle, so to speak. Harry could possibly alleviate her suffering much more quickly than going through emergency services, but did he dare? He couldn't know what was happening to Bakari unless he directly observed what was happening in her brain. Normally, he would never push his way into a person's consciousness without their permission. Unfortunately, Bakari wasn't able to give her consent. He was sure he was right, and felt he had no choice but to invade her brain in order to determine what was hurting her. What was she seeing that was so terrifying?

Having made his decision, Harry tentatively extended his thoughts to her, searching for a way to connect. Her distress was so intense that his first attempt bounced off, as if she was generating an energy shield around her brain. Harry stopped to consider the implications of breaking through that shield; was what he was about to do effectively brain surgery? He hesitated, but then Bakari began gasping and moaning piteously, and he felt her terror increase. He feared it was becoming possible she could experience a stroke or cardiac arrest if this situation continued to escalate and felt his time to act was becoming shorter. Harry tried to access a view of Bakari's brain again, this time using slightly more forceful energy, with a more directed focus.

He sensed the energy shield slowly give way, then he was past it and achieved an overview of Bakari's brain. He could now see the untold billions of the brain's neurons arcing through its vast network of synaptic pathways. Each synapse connected an individual neuron to another, and those were connected in turn to yet more neurons. Reacting to stimuli, the neurons sent electrical pulses across the long nerve fibers that made up each synapse. Each pulse was an instruction, collectively resulting in innumerable chemical instructions and interactions that would perhaps end in the twitch of a finger, the blink of an eye, or a lifesaving breath. Each instruction was represented by an infinitesimally brief flash of barely discernable pale light. This flashing movement gave Harry the impression of a dense, foggy web of randomly racing pinpoints of light that overlay the brain's entire surface. The individual lights were moving so fast they nearly blended into solid, pulsing lines.

With Bakari basically out of action, though, what stimuli were causing the unusual reactions he was seeing? There were processes in the brain that stimulated autonomic physical reactions, of course—respiration, heartbeat, and the rest—but surely that didn't account for Bakari's current condition. Harry then noticed a very small area of her brain that the light web didn't seem to cover; it appeared dark, inactive. He drew his focus solely to that area to see if perhaps it was damaged. It definitely wasn't inactive; he could see the sluggish, low waves of very low energy pulses slowly traversing the dark area. Harry suspected this area was somehow the genesis of Bakari's hallucinations, and he wanted to see what she herself was seeing in her mind. (Harry had a passing thought of the philosophical debate on brain vs mind but decided that was really too distracting for now.) He extended a single, molecule-wide filament of energy to hover bare microns above the dark area.

Harry took a further chance, and using the barest touch of the energy filament, descended through the lethargically rippling surface to learn what lay beneath it. What he saw stunned him; he couldn't immediately classify it as either vision, hallucination, or memory. He couldn't recall experiencing anything like this other than in his own mind. The scene passing before him seemed as if he had accessed one of his past-life memories, momentarily disorienting him as it invaded and captured his senses. In addition to seeing what appeared before him, Harry could almost hear and feel the actions taking place in the scene, and it was an unfortunate scene indeed. As with his usual experience viewing his own past lives, in this instance Harry was the Observer, watching the memory unfold, while paradoxically also the Experiencer, somehow reliving the actions he was Observing.

Even in this current age of technology, the oldest human question remained: what happens when a human dies? The body ceases to function, but what else occurs? There were a number of human researchers who used technical means to investigate the delta between life and afterlife. Is there a soul that ascends? They measure and weigh the body before and after death to see if there is a difference in mass, which would supposedly tell them that something of substance had left the body. Do the dying "pierce the veil" and become able to remember their past lives? Researchers record the many human near-death experiences that randomly occur to see if they can capture that moment. They connect the dying body to many forms of scanner technology, hoping to see a change in brain wave patterns at the time of death, other than that they simply stop. Harry knew humans thought of the veil as a metaphor, but he knew it was more than that. There had been a few rare times over the ages when his mind had inadvertently brushed against a human's and he had glimpsed something that hid all that came before the person's current incarnation.

In that instant, Harry had perceived the so-called veil as a barely visible space-time barrier, effectively a force field that separated the physical from the metaphysical. Humans often, somewhat poetically, described the veil as an opaque curtain, drifting at the edge of perception. The veil was said to shield human minds that might not have been strong enough to understand their passage from one life to the next. When Harry happened to review his accessible memories of the innumerable lifetimes he had experienced over millennia, he had seen and re-experienced his own death—however temporary—many times. He believed he had never had such a veil in his own mind. Now he watched one of Bakari's deaths and considered the effect of seeing one's death occur when one had no idea what was occurring, or why. Traumatic couldn't begin to describe it; it could take the person beyond fear, into catatonia. Witness Bakari, twitching in her chair, her mind forced elsewhere, her body frozen.

I n the scene before him, Harry saw a boy of about fourteen, his chest and face painted with brilliant yellow and red stripes, riding to the hunt for the first time with his tribe's several dozen experienced hunters. The boy had been placed in the middle of the group, safely behind his eldest uncle. Harry sensed the boy was exhilarated and proud to finally participate with his elders in sustaining the tribe. Harry could hear the whisper of the knee-high grasses that bent under the ponies' hooves as they ran. He could smell the aroma of crushed plants rising in the sun's blistering warmth, and the heated scent of the people as well. The hunters on their ponies raced across a broad plain, where against the horizon could be seen a vast, dark herd of large, hump-backed animals. Each mighty animal had a huge head and short, curved horns thrusting out from each side of the head. Harry couldn't determine where or when this hunt took place, other than his observance of the hunters' appearance and the style of their weapons.

The hunters' skin looked like glistening mahogany, ranging in shade from relatively light to moderately dark; their long, thick hair was uniformly black and left loose to hang to their shoulders. Their simple but strong, well-made bows were slung over their shoulders, and quivers of long, straight arrows hung across their backs, bouncing as they ran their ponies. Harry believed he was seeing the memory of a tribal bison hunt that had occurred in prehistoric times. The hunters—forerunners of cowboys, vaqueros, and such other bovine and equine handlers—stayed to the rear of herd, ready to pick off stragglers with their deadly arrows. This tribe had followed this herd for many of the tribe's generations and would not kill more individuals than were needed. The animals taken today would keep the tribe in food for many months, and provide much material for warm robes, hides to cover dwellings, bones for making everyday implements, and sinews for bowstrings.

The bison herd finally spied the hunters and began running. Harry saw the dense, choking dust cloud raised by the animals, and felt the earth shake with the thunder of their hooves. Suddenly, the pony ridden by the boy's eldest uncle stepped in a hole and fell, snapping its right foreleg and rolling on its side, screaming in agony. The uncle kicked away from his pony as it fell and rapidly rolled clear. Harry watched the uncle quickly jump to his feet and look to the pony, presumably to see if there was anything he could do for it. The other hunters saw the fall and surged wide around him, driving the herd away from the fallen, knowing he would either recover or not. His young nephew inexpertly tried to slow his pony to avoid running into the injured pony, instead of following the other hunters around it. Harry saw the uncle's shock as his nephew's pony stumbled over the injured one and his nephew was thrown to the ground. The boy also tried to kick off and roll as he had been taught, but when he had hit the ground the air was blasted out of his lungs, and his head viciously struck the hard, rocky surface. A wavering darkness crossed the boy's vision as he tried to get to his feet, but he was too stunned to move quickly enough and got no further than his knees.

By foul chance, the herd began to turn and circle behind the hunters. Harry saw the shock on the uncle's face turn to horror as he watched the herd change course to a path that would take it close to the two downed ponies and his nephew. He began running toward the boy, waving his arms and yelling at the animals, hoping the herd would be diverted and run fully clear of the boy. Before the uncle could reach his nephew, a lone bison frantically carved away from the dusty, bellowing mass that the hunters were managing to turn away from the boy and the ponies. The single bison instead turned to run directly toward the boy, moving much faster than the uncle could run. Harry's perspective changed then from observing the scene to experiencing the event with the boy, and he could sense the boy's confused panic.

The boy tried to rise again but the bison was upon him too quickly. Harry felt the boy's terror as the sky above him was darkened by the immense body of the bison, and the smell of the monstrous animal overtook his senses. Harry felt the shadow of the boy's incandescent pain as the animal's heavy hooves broke the boy's legs, then crushed his sternum and flattened his skull. The pain reflected the body's end and was soon over. The dust rose as a thick wave, raised by the pounding feet of the herd as it raced away, to wash over the uncle and the nephew. When the herd had passed and the dust had slowly sifted to the ground, there wasn't much left of the boy for the uncle to gather for the tribe's death rites, but the uncle did what he could.

Harry thought that would be the end, but inexplicably the memory replay began again. This was very unusual in Harry's experience. He was able to easily disengage himself from the repeating experience, but he didn't think Bakari would be able to do it on her own. He thought that whatever malfunctioning element was repeatedly driving the memory through her mind might eventually run out of energy and the images would stop, but possibly not until Bakari's small body was at its final, desperate edge. While her death would resolve the problem, that result was not acceptable. Harry sent a small spark of energy into the dark area, to try to break the repeating cycle. Whatever brain synapses had been frozen, keeping the vision active, were short-circuited. The slow ripples ceased undulating across the dark area, but the energy layer itself remained, inert, floating on the small area like an oil slick on the surface of the ocean. When the death scene abruptly stopped, Bakari gasped once more and her body relaxed, becoming limp. She slowly toppled from the chair to the carpet. On the floor, she curled on her side and seemed to be unconscious.

Harry grimly thought it was no wonder Bakari

believed she was hallucinating these scenes. She had never been given a different possibility and had been told it was a fault in her brain, which had resulted in her being incorrectly diagnosed with schizophrenia. Harry kept his focus on the dark area, realizing that while he had interrupted this episode, there was nothing he could see that would stop memories of her past lives from breaking into her consciousness. While in general seeing past lives could at best be disorienting to the unknowing and untrained human, repeatedly experiencing death of one sort or another would be horrifying. It was doubtful he would be around to help again if her brain re-froze its synapses on another such scene.

He selected a single memory of his own of having glimpsed such a barrier in another human's mind. The remembered image was static, and it wasn't immediately apparent to him how it might have been created, much less sustained. Harry wished he could enlarge what he could see in the static image in his mind, and the image unexpectedly expanded. Harry excitedly tried incrementally enlarging the image, again and again, until he was seeing each individual atom. The result of his mental efforts astonished him. Harry realized he was successfully manipulating his quantum memories in a manner he hadn't known was possible. Perhaps, he thought, there hadn't been sufficient motivation before now.

Harry saw that the barrier was composed of innumerable atoms, each bonded to the next by a form of energy lattice he hadn't seen before. The bonded atoms formed a dense molecular structure he could only presume would deter an unprepared human mind from passing through to the other, nonphysical side. Harry didn't know how such a process would operate. He could discern the specific differences between the barrier energy he could see in his static memory and the somnolent film lying across the surface of the dark area in Bakari's brain. He let go of the static image in his mind and returned his focus to the dark area. Harry could clearly see that the barrier in his memory was created in the same manner as the inert energy he could see before him. One alive, the other seemingly dead, but seeming to be dead wasn't the same as being dead. If he was to alleviate Bakari's suffering, possibly enable her to live a better life, should he take action? Or, as with The People, his beloved, vanished tribe, was he again interfering with the natural order of a being's life?

Harry was a compassionate being and felt he was called upon to help others, human or not, as he could, as he lived each of his lives. To treat others as he would wish to be treated himself. He snorted; Bakari's condition was not a Prime Directive situation, where a species' cultural development was at risk. This was one small, suffering being, helpless to affect a remedy that Harry knew he could perform. If he could help her, he felt compelled to do so. Having made his decision, he placed the tip of the energy filament upon the oily surface of the dark area and poured his energy through the filament until it glowed white-hot but holding it back. Taking a steadying breath, he began slowly releasing the living energy through the filament, into the dark area. He could see it begin to lighten, and gradually to glow. There was an audible crackling sound, and the filament was abruptly thrown aside. The now-living energy suffused the formerly dark area, but it didn't connect itself to the web of light that covered the rest of the brain. Harry didn't know if the result of his effort was sufficient to protect Bakari; although the area now seemed healthy, there was no discernable barrier.

As Harry continued watching the glowing area, he had the oddest sense that it was waking, stretching, reaching out to fill some unknowable corners of reality and other- reality. He saw the glow brighten briefly, then it seemed to suddenly snap into place. Where there had been a useless layer of dull, weak energy, a gently vibrating layer now glowed over the tiny area. No other area of the brain had such a layer. Harry saw that the glowing layer *was* a barrier, had become a veil, and he knew that he had been successful. The barrier was different from anything Harry had experienced, and he was drawn to try touching it, to try to feel its difference. Withdrawing residual energy back into himself, he reached out with his mind to touch the veil. At the instant of connection he was thrown outward, away, and scrambled mentally to regain his equilibrium. He became conscious of his surroundings, and knew that he still stood, although a little shaken, beside his aquarium. He saw that Bakari still lay on the carpet, but still seemed to be unconscious. Harry's head was throbbing, and he checked his eyes and ears to make sure they weren't bleeding. He was, surprisingly, in apparent good order. He thought it was more than time for a nap, but first he had to send another text.

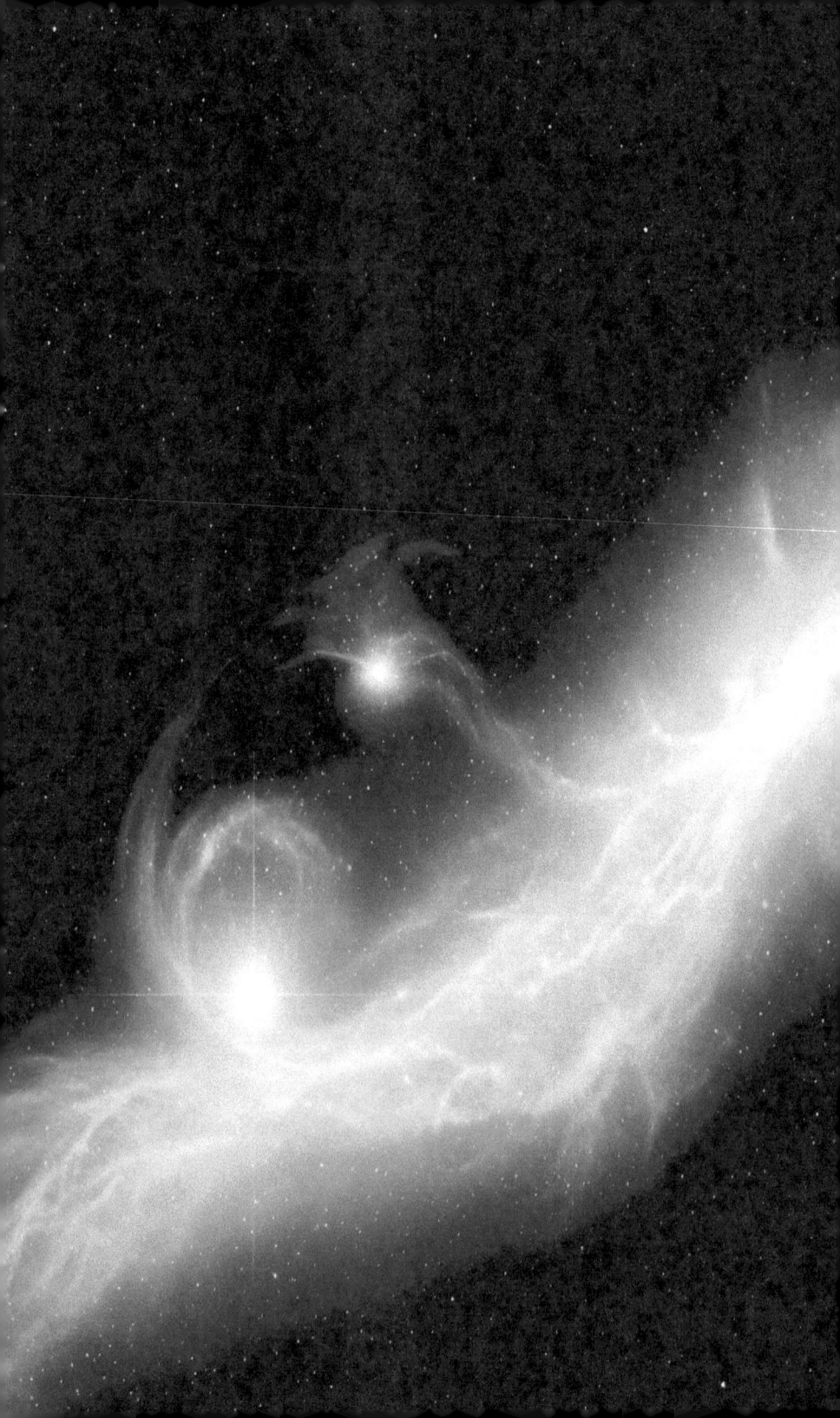

My phone dings with an incoming text alert. I pull it from my pocket as I'm walking out to find what I apparently need to commit a felony. It's from Harry, and I put a move on to go show it to Elena:

"Me again. Listen, things are very calm here and I'm perfectly safe. Everything is fine, I'm not under duress, although I'd have to say that if I actually were under duress, right? lol Like, if the kidnapper was dangerous, which is not (now) the case. Too bad we don't have a code. I do want you to come pick me up, but I don't have the address. You'll need an app for that. I could probably fly home, but I couldn't carry my aquarium. Boy howdy, do I have a story for you!"

I catch up with Elena as she's coming out of the shed, burdened with our rope and duct tape, and unfortunately, she's found a really big flashlight. I'm going to have to keep a closer eye on the type of things stored in the shed, now that I have seen this vengeful angel side of her. I'm walking beside her toward her car, trying to show her the text message but she shrugs my hand off her arm.

"Honestly, Tristan, we don't have time for more foolishness. Harry could be suffering while we dither about what to take and where to go."

She dumps her armload of felony-related equipment on the ground at the back of her car and opens the trunk. I finally stop her by wrapping my arms completely around her so that she can't leave right away. I can feel her entire body shaking. I loosen my hug and show her the phone again.

"Elena, please just look at this, it's a text from Harry. He says he's okay, see? We'll go get him for sure, but let's take the intensity down a notch or two, okay?"

She takes the phone from me and sits on the car bumper while she reads it. Her eyes close briefly and I can see some of the tension leaving her posture. She rubs her face and wipes her eyes. "Do you think this is really from Harry? Someone

could be forcing him to send us these messages, you know." "I do think it's from Harry, and I do think he's okay. I

mean, it's got his snark all over it."

Elena laughs a little and hands the phone back to me. I put it in my pocket and start to gather up the rope and things, keeping a wary eye on her, but she doesn't try to stop me. She stands up and shakes out her arms. She tilts her head to the side and gives a look that tells me she hasn't completely given up on vengeance just yet.

"It's definitely got his snark. So. I'm going to go inside and take a little break while you put that stuff back in the shed, if you would. I'm going to make fresh coffee and take a shower, change my clothes. And then, *mi amigo*, we're going to go pick up Harry."

"Absolutely, we are going to go pick up Harry. Hey, hey—if he can text, I bet he could answer a call! Here, let's try calling him."

The phone rings and rings, but just as I'm about to give up Harry answers.

There was an annoying sound beating on his ears. Harry opened his eyes and saw that Bakari was still lying on the floor near the chair, but she was now breathing regularly and didn't appear to be in distress. Not being a doctor, he couldn't tell if she was unconscious or just asleep. He stood and shook the crinkles out of his legs, then fluttered his wings a bit to get the circulation going there. His wings and muscles were still a little sore, although nothing like being pinned to a board. He shuddered and felt that he should be very angry with Bakari. However, there was too much new information to consider, and he didn't want to take the time or energy to feed anger and revenge. Gradually, he realized that the annoying sound was his phone signaling a call coming in. He flung out his wings and quickly flew into his aquarium, forcefully tapping the icon to answer the call as he scrambled to land in front of the phone.

"Tristan, is that you and Elena?"

Elena grabbed the phone from Tristan and put it on speaker. "Yes, yes, Harry it's us! Are you okay? Are you hurt?"

Harry did a little jig in front of the phone. "I'm fine, really, not hurt at all. There was a little trouble at first but everything worked out. I can explain when you get here." He paused to pat his eyes with his mittens. "You're coming to get me, aren't you?"

Tristan leaned into the phone, speaking loudly. "Of course we're coming, pal. We've got your phone's location mapped and we'll be there in about half an hour. Ah—how are we going to get into the building?"

Harry had to stop and think about that. "I'll see if I can get under the door and go see if the front door is locked. Hang on, don't go away, I'll be right back! Oh—there's no one else here but Bakari, aka Critter!"

I set the Critter revelation aside for the moment. Harry wants to go unlock the front door to make sure we can get in. I need more information first, and yell into the phone for him to stay on the phone but I can hear his wings buzzing, so I assume he's left the aquarium. I rub my forehead in fierce exasperation; there's definitely a headache building up here. My patience is taking a severe beating today. Elena is still holding the phone out so we can both talk into it, and I assume we'll be able to hear him when he comes back. I decide to take a load off and drop onto the couch. Elena gingerly sits beside me, very careful to not accidentally disconnect the call. She looks at me and I can see she's not any happier than I am, but there's not a lot we can do right now. I state the obvious:

"Well, apparently he's gone to unlock the door and we're supposed to hang on here until he's back. He needs to do a better job of listening, in my opinion."

Elena wearily rubs her own forehead. "Let's give him the benefit of the doubt and see what he comes back with. I'm just thankful he's not hurt."

Harry heard some shouting from the phone but he was on

a mission and didn't stop to answer back. He quickly flitted out of the aquarium and flew across the room to the door, dropping down a little to check Bakari with a quick glance to see that she was still sleeping. He landed on the carpet directly in front of the door, where he could see light shining from the other side. He bent down to check the gap between the bottom of the door and the floor, and thought it looked plenty wide enough for him to squeeze through. Harry took a deep breath, then flattened himself to the floor, stretching his legs as far out on each side as he could. He wriggled forward, pushing his head under the door, then his shoulders, but his wing covers stuck. He refused to stop and forced himself forward. There was a concerning creaking sound from his left wing cover, then he was through the gap. He gave an annoyed huff, thinking: *That's going to leave a mark.*

Harry emerged on the other side of the door and stepped into a wide hallway, facing a carved wooden balustrade that fronted a ten-foot drop to the tiled entry floor below. The wooden hallway floorboards had a glossy wax finish and were adorned with a narrow carpet runner. On his left, the hallway led past several more closed doors. A shorter distance to his right led to a staircase that descended to the tiled foyer below, which appeared to be the primary entry to the house. He extended his wings, and sure enough the left wing hung up a bit, but then jerked free. He test-buzzed his wings for a second or two, then launched himself from the top of the staircase. In no time at all, he was hovering before the electronic locking mechanism of the door. He hovered closer to the keypad on the wall beside the door. Harry assumed the keyboard operated the controls for the house alarm system. He didn't really know anything more about alarm systems, but if it could be turned on, he reasoned, it could be turned off. If the alarm was turned off, he assumed surely the door would then unlock.

He considered whether to try something now, or to go back upstairs to report to Tristan and Elena. They might have an idea about how to access the house. On the other mitten, he could try to see if he could disarm the lock himself. He elected to try pressing the button labeled "Off." Nothing happened, and the button labeled "Armed" still showed a green light. The "Off" button seemed to be stuck. Harry mentally weighed the pros and cons:

Hm. I could try giving the system a quick jolt to see if that gets things unstuck. It will either work or not, and no harm done if it doesn't. It's not like I can set fire to the place.

Harry didn't know if he actually had any residual energy with which to produce said jolt, since he really had extended himself in helping Bakari. He'd had enough of this adventure, though, and wanted to go home. He gathered his concentration, and slowly reached toward the keypad.

Suddenly Elena and I hear an unbelievably loud mechanical shriek come from the phone. We both jump and Elena drops the phone on the floor. I manage to get to it first and try to figure out what's going on. I've heard that sound before— it's a home break-in alarm going off. I can also hear a secondary whoop that sure sounds to me like a fire alarm. Whatever lock Harry was trying to check, he's apparently managed to set off a localized Armageddon alert. Elena shouts over the alarms, but of course I can't hear what she's saying. There's nothing for it but to disconnect the call, which I do.

The sudden silence is almost as stunning as the alarms. We look at each other in disbelief. Elena tries again:

"What the holy hell was that? It sounded like an air raid warning—did the place blow up? What do we do now?" "I don't think anything actually blew up, but it appears that a homeowner can ramp up the burglar alarm volume to truly explosive levels. I expect Harry somehow accidentally set off the alarms when he was checking the door lock. Lord only knows what police and fire units will respond to that, but my guess is probably all of them. We'd better go ahead on over there."

Meanwhile:

Over time, while transforming their environment humans found that the electrical power of lightning could be created, and controlled, by other means. Humans generated the electricity that powered modern human culture. Electricity became humanity's cultural friend, but under certain conditions it could be decidedly unfriendly to physical formations, especially when that physical formation was a small, mantis-type being.

The Victorian style two-story house Bakari lived in was situated toward the back of a large lot, with a mature maple tree standing beside the driveway that led to the garage at the side of the house. The house was a much older structure than the surrounding houses in the quiet, small-town neighborhood. Over its near century of existence portions of the stately house had been remodeled, such as the addition of the alarm system. The contractor who installed the alarm system hadn't been careless, exactly, but the twisted wire connecting the keypad to the house wiring could have used one more twist. The microscopic weakness in the connection wasn't dangerous, but when the keypad was activated sometimes a tiny spark jumped across that weakness. A human pressing a button on the keypad might feel that tiny spark as the release of a slight static charge into their fingertip, but there was a different outcome when Harry pressed the " Off" button with a little extra spin.

So it was that Harry's quick jolt met the tiny spark on the other side of the keypad, and the two combined to jump back through the button to meet the still-connected tip of Harry's right mitten. To a human, the energy discharged would have been just a minor static spark, but while Harry was large for a particular type of mantis, he was still a very small being. To him, the effect of the spark was similar to being near a lightning strike; the discharged energy traveled through his body and grounded into the floor. Harry was violently flung backwards across the foyer, where he struck the far wall and slid down it, coming to rest behind a decorative wooden chest standing against the wall. He tried to stand but collapsed to the floor, unconscious.

An unconscious mind is not an inactive mind, however. Harry traveled through his hidden memories to relive the events that would bring him to what he thought of as the "here and now."

PART FOUR

LATE AUTUMN IN THE YEAR OF OUR
LORD, 1349

CHAPTER ONE

The leaves were nearly gone from the trees in the monastery's woodlots. There had not been a killing frost yet, but it was coming. The last monk had died at the end of harvest the previous year and now, another year had passed and it would soon be winter again. The fields and gardens lay fallow. There had been no one left alive to plow or plant; there was no one to harvest the crops or make use of the bounty, had there been a crop. For the one being still living in the monastery, time had not passed quickly, but had stumbled through day after dreary day, month after deadening month.

The small, dark being remained motionless, its many legs tucked as far back as it could manage into a corner of the monastery's refectory ceilihg. He considered his circumstances as he rested. To human eyes, he would appear to be a particular type of largely unloved animal that would eventually come to be known as a tarantula. To his great disgruntlement, he had had no choice in the nature of his current physical body, and because of that body he had been unfairly maligned many times, often dangerously so. He was harmless and non-aggressive, but he could defend himself in dire circumstances. His tiny teeth couldn't bite substances tougher than the skin of berries and leaves, which was fine since he was a fastidious vegetarian. He was fully sentient and highly intelligent, attributes that were severely at odds with humans' automatic assumptions when seeing his current physical form.

He had been called by many names throughout his many long lifetimes, but he was Stalker for now, and had been in his current body configuration for thousands of years. This shadowed corner was his favorite place in the whole of the now-deserted monastery, and he felt himself very lucky to have found it. His shelter in the ceiling rafters was protected from wind and rain by the happenstance of the sturdiness of this portion of the building's exterior wall, onto which a rare, non-leaking portion of the refectory roof remained in place above him. What sunlight there ever was in this damp- benighted country shone through gaps in the opposite stone wall of what had been the monastery dining hall. The only ambient sound to be heard through the heavy, chill air beyond the sinking walls was the rustling of the first bare branches of autumn, and each night was colder than the one before.

The emptiness and silence weighed on him more heavily at night, making his loneliness that much harder to bear. Stalker did not wish to live forever, but he had become resigned to his apparently unending existence within this universe until fate, or the end of time itself, brought an end to his life. Until that end, he would instinctively continue to periodically enter a state of near-non-existence that would last until another type of urge awoke him from his sleep. During his sleep, chemical processes put him into stasis, a state in which he would typically remain for the many thousands of years of each stasis period. As Stalker slept each time, he would continue to change, to evolve from within his own form. While in stasis, his cells would regenerate and evolve at a glacial pace, gradually replacing his pre-stasis attributes with something wholly different, often—but not always— resulting in a new form of being. Over time, through hundreds of thousands of stasis cycles, he had awoken to find himself embodying many different shapes and sizes.

Up to now, Stalker had not felt that instinctual urge to sleep since first awakening in his current form so very long ago. He had wondered on occasion how he might go about initiating stasis at-will, if only as a temporary relief from being alone. He sadly thought once again that it might be best to let himself sleep away the centuries, perhaps even millennia. He thought about his life at the monastery and remembered when Jack the Collier had brought him to the monastery to live with Brother Mark nearly two and half centuries past. Stalker had first met Jack in the dense forest near the local village, when Stalker had been living in a burrow under the roots of an ancient oak tree. His sheltering tree had been felled by village workers, and several tall stacks of branches trimmed from the tree were left behind.

Jack made his livelihood by selling the charcoal he made from such trimmings. Stalker had watched Jack at his work, thinking he was out of the old man's sight, but he learned Jack had sharp eyes. At the end of a particular workday Jack sat beside his small campfire, smoking his pipe, and called to Stalker to come out. Stalker was surprised Jack had spotted him, but warily came out to investigate the interloper. Jack was surprised in turn when Stalker was able to communicate with him using a very basic form of sign language, typically used by traders who didn't speak the local language. Jack had ever had an unusual turn of mind and for him, "conversing" with a non-human filled him not with panic and fear but wonder and delight.

Stalker had had enough of solitary life and wanted to return to the village with Jack, but Jack had been fearful for Stalker's safety should the other villagers happen to cross paths with this unusual small being. As Jack had informed him at the time:

"Ah be a'thinkin', ye see. Ye be not a regular beastie, what w' ye knowin' hand signs and ye bright eyes. Ah doont think ye is a demon, but Ah likely be alone in such thinking. Ah think the villagers might not gie ye time t' hand sign afore killin' ye for a demon.

"Aye. Ah b'lieve there be danger t' ye from the villagers. Ah'm friends w' Brother Mark at the monastery up the way. Ah be of a mind t' take ye t' Brother Mark. Think ye t' travel a ways w' me? Ah ken Brother Mark t'would be a friend t' ye." Jack chuckled and shook his head. "Brother Mark do love the wee beasties."

Stalker had come to love Brother Mark, spending the long, dark winter days secretly learning from everything the monk shared with him, and covertly watching from hiding spots as Brother Mark and his brethren monks transcribed a multitude of books and manuscripts over the years. First Stalker must learn to read, and then there were languages to learn, and history, and geography, and the science of the celestial bodies shining above them, and so much more. This was the sole aspect of Stalker's unique existence that seemed positive to him; he had time to learn. He amassed knowledge with an unending curiosity. During the bright springs and warm summers, Brother Mark worked in the fields and tended the monastery's animals in his own special way. Stalker observed from his usual place sitting on the monk's shoulder, comfortably hidden in the deep cowl of his robe, and learned from this work as well.

The gentle pace of monastery life had seemed timeless, and Stalker had gently relaxed into that rhythm, temporarily forgetting that Brother Mark would fade, just as had all the beings that Stalker had ever observed or known. However, his pain of losing Brother Mark had been assuaged in a loving manner. Brother Mark revealed Stalker to a trusted brother monk, who became Stalker's guardian and mentor upon Brother Mark's passing to join his Lord. The chosen brother took an oath in their Lord's eyes to choose another guardian in turn, and to apply the same oath to his successor. In this way Stalker continued to be protected, taught, and loved during the centuries he lived at the monastery. Brother Mark remained the only monk who had ever been able to speak mind-to-mind with him, and after Brother Mark's passing Stalker was necessarily limited to communicating through "hand signs." This method of communication served its purpose, but Stalker found it incomplete and unsatisfying, and wished for the ability to speak aloud as humans did.

D uring all his thousands of lives, Stalker had seen many things throughout the geologic ages: mountains risen from the raging center of the planet, only to crumble to gravel before rising again; oceans turned to desert, and desert returned to forest. He knew that not everything would rise again and that once gone, some things were gone forever. Stalker had learned with deadening finality that, for other than himself, living beings came to an end and did not return. This understanding did not help him when his peaceful life at the monastery was not spared from utter destruction. His monastic life had changed, over a period of mere months, from one of friendship and fulfillment to a horror of emptiness and ruin. Plague had come to the monastery, not sneaking as a thief in the night but in the warmth of daylight, embedded within a group of seemingly innocent visitors.

As was the custom of the time, a richly dressed noble with his family, several guards and servants had stopped at the monastery to rest before continuing to their destination. The beside the body for a time, until at st he had fled to a far corner of the monastery to face his own solitude.

Stalker now lived a lonely life. His daily routine was rummaging for food through the wildly overgrown berry vines alongside the kitchen garden, then climbing to his lofty refuge as day faded to twilight, then darkness. The nights were very dark these days. Within the monastery, where there would have been the occasional candle gleaming against an interior wall there was nothing but shadow. There was no scent of smoke from evening cook fire or warming braziers, no voices heard echoing down a hallway. All the monks were gone. All the nearby villagers were gone as well, their animals eventually dispersing themselves to increasingly wild forests, to inadvertently feed the local wolves and other predators. The monastery's fields lay chill and fallow, its gardens invisible beneath the returning natural vegetation of the land. He was comforted by the further thought that his beloved Brother Mark, who had left this mortal life so long ago, had not lived to see these current times. Brother Mark had already been far into his later years when Stalker's companion, Jack the Collier, had taken him to the monastery and placed him in Brother Mark's care. Stalker's time with Brother Mark had encompassed too short a time, but that time had been filled with love and devotion to learning.

Now, everything not already dead seemed to be dying, as if the face of the Earth had turned away in despair.

CHAPTER THREE

The sky was just turning to twilight, the first stars gradually becoming visible above the horizon. Stalker was dispiritedly settling in for another long night when he heard swishing noises, as if something was slowly walking through the damp and overgrown kitchen garden just outside the refectory. He listened more closely, scarcely breathing and firmly setting aside any hope. The last time he had heard something like this he had rushed from his ceiling corner to a place where he could look out, hoping to see a living human being at last. There had only been a lone donkey wandering about, tattered remnants of its former owner's belongings still tied to its back. Stalker had assumed the animal found something nourishing among the weeds, since it still wandered the monastery grounds several days later. He thought the sounds must have been caused by the donkey, but now he could hear voices. In his experience non-human animals didn't normally converse aloud in a language understandable to those not of their given species. He dared to creep from his corner to reach an opening from which he could see into the kitchen garden.

Through the slowly deepening darkness, Stalker could make out two shadowy figures making their awkward, noisy way along the side of the building toward the refectory door, which hung crookedly from rusting hinges. He remembered caution in time to shrink away from his open viewing spot just as the door was slowly pushed open, the hinges making a hideous screech. The two figures paused in the doorway to survey the interior. Stalker assumed they wanted to make sure there was no immediately obvious danger. After this recon-noiter the two advanced into the center of the room, and with relieved groans dropped their traveling packs to the dusty wooden plank floor. They followed the packs to the floor, sitting cross-legged with apparent exhaustion. One of the monks was just a little taller than the other, but neither of them was a large man. Both were starvation-thin, and their robes were little more than a collection of worn spots held together with more hope than wool.

The two remained seated this way for several moments, then one wearily reached into his pack and retrieved a string of beads. Stalker's heart leaped when he recognized the rough wooden cross hanging among the beads. Could it be that these two were monks, looking for their brothers? Stalker murmured his own prayer along with the one saying his rosary, ending with a silent *amen* as the man finished this rite. It wasn't the same as the glorious chants the monastery's brothers had sung at vespers over the centuries, but it caused Stalker to realize with shock that he had not prayed since the last monk had died. He considered the small, warm spot he felt in his heart and knew this was a small grace he needed to allow himself each day again. He shook off his musings when the man patted the shoulder of the other, who seemed to have fallen asleep where he sat, and began speaking in a low, soft voice.

"Come now, Brother Eustace, we must order ourselves for the night. I will see if we might not have a wee fire within the presumed safety of these lonely walls."

Brother Eustace shook his large, shaggy head and rubbed his eyes as he straightened his long legs in front of him. "Aye, I am that tired for sure, to have missed evening prayers with you. Are we alone here after all, Brother Alwin? I had hoped some others would also have been spared."

Brother Alwin tucked his rosary away beneath the front of his robe and looked around the increasingly shadowed room. "It would seem for now there are no others, sadly. It is past sunset now and the light is too dim for us to search the buildings, but there does not seem to be any sign of life. Well, other than our weary selves and that poor stray donkey we saw just outside. Perhaps we will travel to the village tomorrow to see if anyone there yet lives. We have a dire need for food." He sighed deeply. "We have been lucky in our travels thus far, but now we face the coming winter months when finding food becomes a fearful task. We shall then see if the plague has not killed us after all but is just taking a much longer time to do so."

After a further moment spent surveying the room, Brother Alwin tiredly dragged his traveling pack onto his lap and began to rummage through it, eventually removing the carefully wrapped, thick stub of his precious tallow candle, which he placed upright on the floor. Another quick search through the pack brought forth a leather pouch that held various dried materials, such as moss, several pieces of straw, and thin slivers of tree bark, together with his flint and his much-loved iron fire striker. Except for a single piece of straw and the striker, the rest was set aside for the moment. Holding the fragment of straw firmly atop the flint, the monk sharply struck the edge of the flint with the iron striker, and a crumb of hot spark caught on the straw. Alwin carefully applied the smoldering end of straw to the candlewick, gently blowing on the resulting tiny flame to encourage it. He gave a satisfied grunt and shielded the lighted candle with his hand as he stood and turned to peer more closely into the farther areas of the increasingly dark room.

"While I do confess to the sin of being attached to worldly possessions, it is a blessing to have the use of such a simple tool. This small bit of brightness is not much, but we shall have light enough to see if we can find the wherewithal to furnish ourselves with the means for a much larger light, not to mention warmth."

Despite the eerie shadows cast by the dim, wavering candlelight, the monks were able to see that some semblance of the refectory's usefulness remained in place: the fireplace at the end of the room had not fallen apart; there was a chance the chimney was not blocked, and there was even a small stack of firewood arranged beside it; and a long wooden table and bench stood along the wall nearest the fireplace. Brother Alwin gestured to the firewood with a small laugh and handed the lit candle to Brother Eustace.

"It seems we shall not freeze, at least not this night. I shall arrange the beginnings of a fire if you will guard our precious light a few moments."

Brother Eustace grunted assent as he took the candle guardianship. Alwin located the simple iron poker lying beside the hearth and used it to inelegantly push a part of the accumulated ash pile to the side of the fireplace. The damp air had caused the ash to become compacted; moving it was akin to moving heavy, unwieldy stones. After a few minutes of strenuous effort, he had made a sort of pit that, luckily, was dry at the bottom and commenced a search for something resembling kindling. The floor under the wood stacked nearby provided a fund of the usual detritus of a log pile, and the small chips of bark and splinters were quickly gathered and placed in the pit. Brother Alwin stood aside and brushed ash from his hands and robe. Brother Eustace had taken his charge to guard their light very seriously and had stood nearly motionless while these preparations were underway. Now he stepped forward and very carefully applied the candle flame to the tinder, holding it steady until a larger flame jumped to life. Smaller pieces of wood were carefully laid on the crackling bed of tinder, each coming aflame in turn. Eventually the fire could support the split lengths of logs that would burn throughout the night, warming the area in front of the fireplace. The monks retrieved their packs from the farther shadows of the room and withdrew the threadbare blankets they used for bedding. The wooden floor was hard but dry. They removed their damp, thin-soled leather shoes and placed them to the side of the fireplace. Each of them sat silently on his blanket close to the fireplace, watching the flames leap about. The crackling and hiss of the burning wood were the only sounds to be heard. Brother Alwin shook himself and clapped his hands together very lightly, then rustled about in his own pack for a moment.

"My good Brother Eustace, I believe a small celebration is in order. We have a roof over our heads and the warmth of a fire at our feet. And—I have here a treat that we shall share before we go to our sleep." He drew out a large apple, sound but withered, and held it up to catch the firelight.

Brother Eustace chuckled and dragged his pack into his lap. "And I have here—just a moment, if you will—I have here the very implement required for this celebration." He produced a small, well-used knife with a significantly nicked edge and handed it to Brother Alwin. "If you will do the honor, my friend, I will happily accept your beneficence. We were for a fact well-met along the road to this sad place. You are a most satisfactory traveling companion."

Brother Alwin smiled as he cut the apple in half and offered it to Brother Eustace to take first choice. "As are you. We were fortunate indeed to have met in our search for our brethren. I despaired of seeing another living person until I saw you walking ahead of me on the road this past fortnight."

They blessed their food and paused to savor their small meal, taking tiny bites and making each one last as long as they could. No part of the apple was wasted, and although it was finished too soon, it had tasted sweetly of past good fortune. A few swallows from their waterskins finished their feast. Eustace shook his head as he returned his waterskin to his pack.

"I felt the same despair. I have found during my long months of wandering that placing one foot in front of the other down a solitary path provides much opportunity for reflection upon these times. In the face of such terrible suffering, I asked our Lord why do some live, when so many others do not? Why did my fever break, but all of my flock perished from their fevers, and much worse agonies besides? Unhappily, I have obtained no answers to my questions. My faith in our Lord remains strong, but I confess I do not understand His plan, why He seems to need so many souls at once. In my innocence I did not think there was evil enough in the world to warrant such apocalyptic punishment. I have since thought that perhaps it was not innocence on my part but rather arrogance, and my punishment is to remain behind."

Alwin shook his head in turn. "I also broke the fever and lived through the agonies of the sores. I tried, I mightily tried, but I could not save anyone in my parish, no one at all. All are gone, from the eldest to the very youngest. All are gone except for me. I rose from my bed and dug graves until I could not lift the shovel, and there were still those waiting in their shrouds. I dug and dug, until there were no more shrouds. Then I had no reason to stay. I thought I would travel to the closest monastery and find comfort there, but all were dead, many of them still in their beds. It was the same everywhere, from the smallest parish church to now this monastery. For many weeks I walked, and I saw no one living until I saw you. Even so, I believe we were spared for a reason, although we do not yet know the nature of that reason."

Eustace arranged his pack as a pillow, then laid down on his back and with a heartfelt groan, stretched his legs out toward their small fire. "I cannot find a purpose in this misery. The number of dead from this pestilence seems to outpace all the dead of war combined."

Alwin spread his worn blanket on the floor beside Eustace and sat staring into the flames. "It is very hard, I know, but do not lose your faith, my friend. Have faith that we have not been abandoned by our God. Have faith that with our Lord there is always a purpose, even though we may not be able to understand what that purpose might be."

He wearily rubbed the top of his head, feeling the stubble that was gradually replacing his tonsure. He worried that he hadn't kept his tonsure trimmed appropriately during his travels, and that this very visible aspect would make it appear his faith was weakening. He noted that Eustace's tonsure was in the same ragged condition and feared that Eustace's faith was becoming ragged as well. Alwin arranged himself for sleep and gave some thought to heavenly punishments.

S talker woke well before dawn, as was his habit. He recalled the visitors below him and settled back into the shadows to observe them as they also began stirring, moving slowly to rise from the hard floor. The one called Alwin took out his rosary and bowed his head, saying his brief morning prayers. Eustace didn't have a rosary but joined his voice with Alwin's. In this situation, there was no litany or chant to soothe them all. Stalker remembered to say his own prayer and realized that it was a hopeful thing to give thanks for things as simple as light and breath. He listened to the two begin discussing their plans to leave this day; he had been hoping they might stay longer. He dared to move along the ceiling rafter to where he was very nearly above their heads, being sure to stay within the shadows.

Alwin shook the floor's dust from his blanket and placed it in his travel pack. He smiled cheerfully at his companion and leaned back to stretch his spine.

"Well, Eustace, my old bones are stiff, but I do say this floor was better than the damp forest floor. I wonder if we might not salvage something from yon kitchen garden. There may yet be a potato or onion left for the scavenging."

Stalker lifted his front legs in amazement upon hearing this comment. He remembered the several small storage cupboards in an alcove off the kitchen, but he didn't know if the visitors would know to look for supplies, given the generally decrepit condition of the monastery buildings. He had spent decades watching the monks as they carried out their tasks to keep body and soul together: planting and harvesting their food; raising livestock; shearing sheep, spinning wool, then weaving the wool into the material from which they made their robes; and the much heavier, denser weaving for their blankets. He knew where such things were stored for future needs. He knew where there was a rosary that Eustace could have. He knew where the wax-sealed jar of honey stood, and where any remaining provisions could be found. He thought all these things were probably still in storage, as all his brother monks died so quickly and no one else came to the monastery after that. No one had walked the worn path from the village to the supposed safety of the hospice. After the first travelers who had fled inland from the coastal city, no others had appeared from along the forest paths.

He had been lost in his memories and was startled to realize the two brothers below were in the process of leaving the refectory. He had to stop them, to let them know there could be aid here! He didn't dare try directly communicating clear thoughts to them, as he would have done with Brother Mark. Over the dozens of decades Stalker had lived with the brotherhood, his ability to communicate by thought had been a carefully kept secret, and he had communicated with his succession of guardians using only hand signs. Stalker's guardianship had been passed from sympathetic brother to sympathetic brother over time, as each friend had faded away to finally join their Lord. The two brothers moving around below his hidden perch were not part of that particular monastic brotherhood.

Stalker feared that if he tried communicating with them mentally, these brothers might be frightened that ghosts, or worse, emissaries of Satan himself, were reaching into their minds. Instead of sending his thoughts, he focused on an image of the kitchen storage cupboard and gently pushed it into Alwin's mind. Alwin froze in the process of hefting his travel pack over his shoulder.

"Eustace, I have had a very surprising thought just now. Let us investigate this place before we leave. We may find something useful that the poor brothers who lived here may have put aside. I do not think they would mind sharing with us, given our desperate need."

Eustace frowned. "What have you in mind? All those here before us have died, presumably from the plague. We were both spared once and may not have that luck a second time. Dare we trust our wellbeing to their leftovers?"

"I do not fault your caution, my friend, but it matters little whether we die of plague or starvation. While I look forward to joining our Lord in his heavenly realm, I am not hurrying toward that end. All things have their time. It has been nearly a full turn of the seasons since the plague first swept all away before it. If we do not remove things from sleeping chambers we should fare well. We must have food, and we may find that some small portion was put by against future need."

Eustace nodded at this, and his frown became a grimace. "I hear the sense in your words. This monastery, while small, is a wide-spread place and such items could be stored anywhere.

Do you also have any thoughts about where we should look? If we are to leave today we cannot spend the whole of the day searching and then not be able to find a secure resting place before nightfall."

Alwin nodded. "I agree, we must be secure before nightfall. It is not likely we will find anything, but I feel we can afford to spend a short time looking. You are correct that it would be too much to search all the grounds. I think we would be best served by seeing if perhaps there might be some sort of storage close to this room. As this immediate area is a place for taking meals, not preparing them, we shall turn our attentions to the kitchen, which I believe is through that doorway." He gestured to a dim doorway at the far end of the large room where they had slept by the fireplace.

Stalker was gratified to see the two move toward the kitchen area, located behind the refectory's dining area. He carefully and quietly scrambled to another rafter in order to keep the monks in sight. He saw them enter the kitchen and stop to investigate the huge, cold fireplace set into the back wall. Alwin quickly spotted the storage cupboard and opened it. Eustace came to stand beside him and halted abruptly upon seeing the cupboard's contents. The cupboard shelves held just a few items, from a small, sealed earthenware jug to several bags in varying sizes, each made from roughly woven cloth and tied at the top with a thick woolen thread. The shelves and storage bags alike were covered with a thick layer of dust, undisturbed by prior searchers.

The grateful monks found two small sacks containing leathery strips of an unidentifiable dried meat, and another that held dried apples. A very small bag held a precious measure of salt. Sitting on the cupboard floor was a somewhat larger bag that held what appeared to be flour; it was also apparent that mice or other creatures had gotten through the bottom of the bag.

"Look here, Eustace. I see that the flour at the top of the sack does not appear to be spoiled by the mice and their compatriots. We may be able to make use of some portion of this if we can find a vessel in which to carry it. What have you there?"

Eustace was investigating the strips of dried meat, sniffing at them and frowning again. "These appear to be unspoiled, but I cannot say from what animal they originated."

Alwin chuckled. "I believe the monastery would have had the usual sheep and cows, and probably chickens and geese as well. Perhaps pigs, and there are always rabbits and deer in the forest. I do not think there is cause for alarm at what sort of creature gave its life in order for our brothers in the Lord to create those provisions."

Eustace's expression remained troubled for another reason. "My friend, do we take all of this, or leave some behind for other travelers who may happen upon this place? There is really not much here, although it serves as a windfall for our needs."

Alwin paused in his own search and gave his full attention to the question. "It is a sad truth that those in desperate need can sometimes be greedy, but I don't think either of us is currently experiencing that affliction. I think the more pertinent question is how can this food best be distributed? Do we leave a portion here in anticipation that someone may happen upon it after we have left, or do we take it with us, in the hope of ministering to the needy that we happen upon in our travels? What is our best course in service to the Lord?"

His companion mused over these moral questions while continuing to search the rest of the cupboard. "My first thought is that if we leave some of the food here, the likelihood of it being found seems too random. However, if we were to take it all with us, we could be assured of having it available to help others. Given that we are making our way eastward to the port city, the chances that we will encounter other travelers with similar need seems to be greater than the possibility of the remainder being found here."

He sighed tiredly but continued his reasoning. "As unlikely as it seems, I admit it is possible others have survived the pestilence. They might look to this place for help, as we have. I think it would be good to leave something here for them, even if there is but a small chance of it being found. As we travel from here, if we happen across those who need our help we could still share whatever we may have with them."

Alwin vigorously nodded his head in agreement. "We are in accord, then. We will divide this bounty, just as our Lord divided the loaves and fishes among the multitude. We will take a portion with us and leave the rest here for other travelers such as ourselves. As you say, as we travel we shall share whatever we have, however meager it may be, with those in need."

Having resolved this apparent moral conflict in a satisfactory manner, the monks set about making their division of supplies. In addition to taking only half of the dried meat strips, the monks carefully divided the dried apples and salt as well. Alwin placed their share of the apples into the sack containing the dried meat and folded their measure of salt into a small piece of cloth torn from his robe, which he tightly bound with the end of a thread from one of the other sacks. He tucked this small parcel in with the dried foods. Eustace was engaged in investigating the contents of the small, sealed jug. A smile finally broke his scowl when he realized the jug held honey that appeared to be of a very fine quality. This discovery led to a spirited discussion of the best way to divide the honey, absent any other similar container. The brothers decided that given that lack, they would take the jug with them but resolved they would be careful to use no more than half its contents for themselves.

Their spirits just a little lighter, the two monks had turned to leave the alcove when Eustace noticed a larger bundle that had gotten pushed far back into the shadowy interior of the lower-most shelf of the cupboard. He drew it out, coughing and waving the resulting dust cloud from in front of his face. A well-loved rosary fell to the floor at his feet, and when he unfolded the bundle he saw that it was a robe and blanket that appeared worn but clean. He held the items up for Alwin's inspection.

"Do you think we might take these as well? There is only one of each, but we can later determine which of us needs which item the more."

Alwin lifted the rosary from the floor and held it out to Eustace. "Please, I think it would be good for you to have this. Yours has been missing a long time, and I know you have greatly felt its loss. I know I depend on my rosary to help anchor me in my faith and I would have you feel the same security."

He laughed then and felt the weave of the woolen robe and blanket. "I think these are not so very much better than our current belongings, but perhaps with fewer holes overall. We shall take them with us and leave behind our gratitude to our brothers who are sadly no longer able to make use of these things. When we stop for the night, we shall see which of us can make the better use of which item, what say you? Ah, is that a smile I see?"

Eustace ducked his head sheepishly. "Aye, I have seen little to smile about these days and I admit to being a grim companion. This day seems to show our fortunes may be afforded a slight improvement from time to time."

Alwin refolded the robe and blanket, then gently gripped Eustace's shoulder. "You are right that these are indeed grim days. We will take these things with us, but let us also take away a measure of hope as well. Our Lord travels with us, as long as our hearts are open to His words."

CHAPTER FIVE

Stalker had never thought of himself as necessarily being religious, nor had he ever been completely convinced that Brother Mark's Lord was his Lord as well. He had followed the monks' teachings, but not so much in their figurative footsteps. Stalker had found deep comfort in the rhythms and rites practiced in the monastery; if pressed, he would have said that his faith was in the ability of the brotherhood to lead others to that comfort. He thought there likely was a higher being with whom all souls endeavored to eventually join. He had no doubt that he had a soul, as he understood the monks' lectures about the soul, but he had no idea whether his soul was like a human soul or was something completely different. He didn't think such a distinction really mattered, but he feared it was possible to lose one's soul. Stalker had unconsciously enrobed himself in his guilt, anger, and distress, and had assumed that every intelligent being still suffering in this disaster could only feel as he felt. He had decided that he, along with all other Earthly beings, had been betrayed by the monks' Lord.

As he eavesdropped on the discussion between the two monks while they investigated the cupboard and made their various decisions, he was surprised, and truthfully a little resentful, to hear the one called Brother Alwin talk about faith and hope. Stalker had lost his faith when he helplessly sat by the bed of the monastery's last monk to die of the pestilence. He had given in to despair and had thought he wanted nothing more than to go to sleep forever. What right did this, this— stranger—have to speak of hope when it seemed to him that he, the two men, and the poor donkey in the garden were all that remained of anything living as far as could be seen or heard?

But as Stalker listened, he knew that hearing human voices in regular discourse was something he desperately needed. He needed it to drown out the lingering memory of the moans and anguished cries of the sick and dying, and to fill his mind with anything other than the all-pervasive silence in which he currently existed. Was hope fulfilled if one didn't know one hoped in the first place? Was it possible the Lord's grace was returning? He didn't know the answers to such questions and was tired of the futile wondering. He knew it was time to take control of his future; it was time to leave the monastery.

It was all well and good to make that decision, but implementing it was a completely different prospect. Stalker contemplated the advisability of trying to establish with these monks the kinds of communication he'd had with Jack the Collier or with Brother Mark. For one thing, he felt he lacked the mental fortitude and emotional energy to get through such a risky endeavor. As well, such an effort takes time, and the monks were already leaving the kitchen area with their supplies. He would be out of time if he didn't act quickly. The monks were back in the refectory now, adjusting their packs to accommodate their newly acquired supplies. Stalker ran across the room's ceiling and over the wooden support beams as fast as he could, ignoring shadows where he would normally stop to check his surroundings to see if it was safe to continue. He discarded all the rules of safe travel in favor of speed, but the monks were already by the door. He had to find a way to stop them, or to at least slow them down. Desperate, he did the only thing he could think to do.

He sent both monks the quick impression that their packs were suddenly far too heavy and bulky to carry. The men staggered a little, puzzled looks on their faces, but they adjusted the packs on their shoulders and continued walking toward the door. Stalker saw his ploy had not been completely effective and increased the mental impression of their packs' weight and bulk just a tiny bit further. The brothers stopped, just inside the door, took the packs from their shoulders, and set them on the floor. Brother Eustace stretched his back, frowned deeply, and bent to check his pack, muttering unhappily as he began rearranging its contents.

"I would not have thought that so few lightweight things would be so heavy when put together. It does not seem reasonable to me that woolens would weigh as much as bricks. It is very strange, very worrisome, almost as if the ghosts of the plague dead do not want us to leave this place."

Brother Alwin, also frowning, was shuffling the things in his pack. "My dear brother, I do not think ghosts of any sort are working against us. I believe we remain under our Lord's protection. However, I must agree that the situation is indeed very odd. I do not understand how our packs suddenly became so heavy. If they are too heavy to carry then we have no choice but to leave some things behind, although it would grieve us sorely to do so."

This was not the result Stalker had foreseen. He had wanted only to slow the two down so he could catch up to them, even though he didn't know what he would do when he had caught up. He didn't want them to leave behind the meager supplies they so clearly needed. He must come up with another option before they had their packs unloaded. At that moment, he heard the donkey moving about in the kitchen garden outside the door and locked onto that mental image. Eustace gasped and his hand flew up to rub his temple. Stalker winced; that sending had definitely been too forceful. "Why, Eustace, whatever is the matter? Have you a

pain?" Alwin looked very concerned, nearly frightened. The specter of extreme, sudden illness was never far from their minds. "Here, you must sit down on this bench."

Eustace permitted Alwin to take his arm and guide him to a bench pushed against the wall near the fireplace. Once seated, he waved a hand to deter Alwin's further ministrations.

"I am well, please do not concern yourself. I shall be fine with just a small sip of water."

Alwin quickly fetched one of their full waterskins from their pile of belongings and handed it to Eustace. His companion took a mouthful of water and resealed the container. He wiped a few errant drops from his lips and gave Alwin a wary look. Stalker watched them anxiously from where he had concealed himself just above their heads.

"Brother Alwin, I had a surprising thought just then, just as you had a thought earlier about the supplies. I had heard what I think was the stray donkey outside, and I wondered if we might not make use of its strong back for a time to carry our packs. Would such usage constitute stealing the animal from the monastery, do you think?"

Alwin gave this careful consideration. "It appears to be a stray animal that could belong anywhere. I was not able to see it clearly in the evening light, but I think it had some remnants of tattered baggage hanging from its harness. I fear its owner may have fallen to the plague somewhere along the road. If we can do nothing else, we should at least free it from that encumbrance before we take our leave of this place. Even though it is a member of that ever so stubborn species, we can hope it may be tractable. If you are feeling better, perhaps we should go introduce ourselves to it."

They rose from the bench and went out through the refectory door, into the sunlit garden. Stalker felt immense relief and began to work his way downward to the floor from his perch in the chill ceiling rafters. He could hear the men coaxing the donkey to come to them and commenting on the rope that was wrapped around it. They determined it would take them some time to get the donkey free of its current lashings and then secure their own baggage for it to carry. The donkey seemed to be remarkably willing to be coaxed, which Stalker could scarcely believe. He had had many experiences with donkeys, and his main memory was of their brazen disregard for common courtesies. He thought the donkey probably hungered for human companionship as much as he did.

In the meantime, Stalker needed to find a place within the monks' baggage in which he could travel unseen with them. He feared to huddle in the bottom of a pack, since the brothers would be going through the packs from time to time during the day and emptying them completely when encamped for the night. It would be difficult for him to remain unseen in those conditions. His only immediate option was to hide in one of the packs and wait for an opportunity to relocate to a hiding place less perilous, but he decided he would do whatever he needed to do in order to leave the monastery. There was no longer an acceptable life for him here, and to head out under his own power would be foolhardy at best. He was good at finding food and hiding, but not much good at all at traveling using his own legs, despite their multiplicity.

With that resolved, he scurried down the closest wall, pausing at the base before crossing the broad expanse of wooden floor. The monks had left their packs just inside the door, but for a small being that was far away. From outside, he could hear the monks' feet trampling along with the donkey's as they returned to the doorway. They would be back in moments. Stalker threw caution to whatever breeze could catch it and darted into the open. He ran as fast as all his legs could manage, not wasting time in lurching from shadow to shadow for cover. He put every bit of his strength into racing across the last few inches in front of him, making it under the folded-over top of a pack just as Alwin stepped through the door. Stalker didn't think he had been seen, but as he gasped for air he worried he might have been heard scrambling inside the pack.

Seemingly unaware of the passenger in his pack, Alwin bent down and lifted the pack that Stalker had just lunged into, giving it a good shake to settle the contents. This jostled Stalker all the way to the bottom of the pack, which wasn't ideal. There were a number of heavy objects in the pack, any of which could be damaging to a being's slender, well-formed leg. Stalker dodged and huddled as best he could, eventually tucking himself into a fold of the blanket. He could hear the muffled, soothing voices of the monks as they worked with the donkey. It seemed that Alwin had more experience with donkeys than Eustace was showing.

"Eustace, perhaps you could hand me that bit of rope hanging just there from Friend Donkey's bridle. No, no, do not pull off the bridle, we shall need it to reconnect the rope for a harness..."

Despite his anxiety over his traveling circumstances, Stalker was greatly amused at the tone of enforced patience in Alwin's voice. He heard a solid thump and Eustace yelped.

"Now, now, Friend Donkey, that is no way to treat our Brother Eustace. You must learn to watch your feet and kicking is not permitted. We must settle our differences amicably. Let us try the bridle again. Eustace, perhaps if you were to step away for a moment and stop flapping your arms, Friend Donkey would be less inclined to misplace his hoof."

Stalker could hear Eustace's exasperated muttering as he moved aside and felt it was time to assist the monks. He found the dim glow of Friend Donkey's mind and sent a gentle, calming message.

"Hello, my friend. Do not fear us. We wish your help and would ask that you permit us to use your strong back for a time."

The donkey shook its long ears and stamped a hoof but otherwise didn't respond to Stalker's overture of friendship. Stalker remembered that in general, such animals didn't communicate mind to mind very well; their thoughts were more foggy expressions of intent and want rather than clear statements. He felt the tension of misery that rose from the donkey's mind. It didn't seem to be hungry, having found adequate foraging in the monastery's grounds, nor was it thirsty. But it was confused and very, very unhappy. It was a domesticated animal and was unnerved by the lack of humans in the countryside. It had wandered randomly, on its own since its last human had staggered to a stop and fallen down in the middle of an empty village. The donkey had stood nearby its human for a long time, but the human didn't rise. Eventually the donkey had fled the horde of opportunistic scavengers that had shown up. Its life since then had become so strange that while it did want companionship, it automatically mistrusted these humans and danced away from their efforts to harness it.

Stalker could sense the donkey's hazy question as to what Stalker was, since he clearly wasn't human. He reached out again, but this time he also used images to convey his thoughts.

"I am but a very small passenger in one of these bundles. These humans are not harmful, however inept one of them appears to be. I think you need our companionship, as we need your strength. Will you help us? These humans are kind and would treat you well."

The donkey lowered its head and permitted Alwin to replace the bridle over its head. Stalker heard Eustace grunt in surprise. "So, the daft animal recognizes its masters at last."

Stalker frowned at that sentiment, but Alwin stepped in to gently correct Eustace. "Brother Eustace, we are not truly the masters of any living thing in this world. We spend much of our time in the struggle to master ourselves. At best we are guides, for both our human and animal charges. The things that give us trouble also help us learn how to better serve our Lord, and we must use patience when faced with adversity. We have been sorely tried, you and I, very sorely tried indeed. Let us try to find some good, any good, that can help us. Such as the good in Friend Donkey here before us."

Eustace replied in what Stalker thought was a shamefaced tone. "I hear your words, Brother Alwin. I do lose sight of my faith from time to time, and the sorrow of that loss comes out in ways I do not intend. I thank you for your patience with me, and I shall attempt to be patient in turn with this unbiddable donkey."

It was the work of only another hour to get the donkey properly harnessed and the packs secured to its back. Neither monk had thought of riding the donkey; it was small, and they worried about its overall health. The brothers planned to travel to the eastern port city that was the home of the cathedral that was in turn the home of their order in this country. They each prayed to themselves that they were not, in fact, the last of their order. They hoped to find other survivors, and perhaps even a reason for this seemingly universal suffering.

PART FIVE
PRESENT DAY

We quickly gather up jackets, wallet, purse, and keys and go out to Elena's car. I'll have to remember to tell her she was right about not using my truck. I have a feeling we want to be as unobtrusive as we can be, given that Harry has done an awesome job of really lighting up the place. I make sure the felonious assault tools are all out of the car, then jump in and start it up. I check to make sure Elena's got her seatbelt fastened; it's just an automatic thing I do when there's a passenger beside me. I notice that her hands are shaking and put my hand over hers to give it a gentle squeeze.

"Listen, Harry wasn't injured when we talked to him just now and we know where he is. We won't dally at all getting there, but we don't need to do a fast and furious routine, either."

That gets a little smile from her, and she seems to relax back into her seat a little as I start the car and quickly back out of the driveway, onto the street. The nice GPS lady alerts me to make a few initial turns, then we're headed southeast down the highway to the small town where Harry's phone is located.

It takes us about ten minutes longer than planned before the GPS lady informs us our location is ahead on our left. We can see an ambulance parked in the house's driveway and a firetruck parked in front of it. There are two police cars as well. The street isn't blocked off, but I don't have a choice other than to slow the car to a crawl to get past all the activity. I continue down the street for a couple of blocks then pull over and put the car in Park, leaving it running. We look back toward the house and see a person on a gurney being put into the ambulance. The police officers appear to have finished questioning the neighbors and the fire truck is pulling out, so it looks like things might be wrapping up. Elena slumps in her seat and rubs her eyes.

"Tristan, I'm sure that's the correct place, but I can't imagine what's going on."

Unfortunately, I can imagine all too well. With a sigh, I lower my forehead to rest on the top of the steering wheel; things just keep getting more and more complicated. "Well, I expect that when Harry tried to use the keypad to unlock the door, the security system called for help. I think the person put in the ambulance must have been Critter. I just hope Harry is still in the house and that he's still okay." I don't say it, but things are feeling pretty grim.

Elena twists around to get a better look through the back window of the car. I lift my head from the steering wheel and adjust the side mirror to watch behind us as the ambulance departs, lights on but no siren. The police officers to their separate patrol cars and also head out. Elena faces front again and taps her fingers on the door handle.

"We have to get inside that house somehow and look for Harry."

My head hurts. "You're right, I don't like it but I agree with you. We're going to have to wait until things have settled down more, though. I'm going to drive around for a few minutes and then we'll see what it looks like. If no one is still outside gossiping, we'll try to get into the house. Maybe you could look up the penalties for breaking and entering just so we know what we're dealing with. It's not going to do Harry any good if we're both in jail."

She takes out her phone and starts a search, looking very serious. "I'll look up lawyers, too. We can use my savings as bail money."

I sigh, put the car into *drive* and check the side view before pulling away from the curb. I really, really don't want to go to jail, whether we have bail money or not.

I drive toward the highway for a few minutes, then head back to the neighborhood. We end up in an alley that runs along the back of the row of houses that includes the one showing up on the GPS. This alley is apparently where the residents put out their trash and recycling for pickup. It's late afternoon now, and it looks like the neighborhood has settled back down from the earlier excitement. I'm grateful that it's a football Sunday, because the second set of games is just about to start. There is no one, and I mean no one, who doesn't watch the home team play, especially when it's a home game like today. That means people will be inside for the most part, so there will be a lot fewer potential witnesses to the break-in we're planning. I park the car parallel to the back of the property and turn off the engine. We sit there for a couple of minutes, quietly observing the area.

There's no fence across the back, which surprises me a little. I guess the crime rate here is pretty low. Up to now, of course. I scope out the back door, which is a few yards away across a smallish back yard that runs up to a nice deck. This house does not belong to poor people. Elena pulls a large flashlight out of her tote bag. I thought I had taken all the burglar tools away from her, but apparently not.

"Elena, it's broad daylight, unfortunately for us, just what do you need a flashlight for?"

The fierce, stubborn look is back, but she tries for a reasonable tone. "Do we know that there's no one in the house? No, we don't. We don't know that all the lights are working, either."

"Even if someone is there, I'm not going to let you bash them with that flashlight. We can't afford to add assault to breaking and entering."

She ignores that and gets ready to get out of the car. "I don't plan on bashing anyone, but I do plan to look in every crack of that house until we find Harry."

I want Harry back just as much as Elena, but I can't help worrying. I get out of the car and join her on the passenger side, where we stand looking over the situation—so I guess we're casing the joint. The shrubbery and trees in this and the neighbors' back yards provide decent privacy, which is to our advantage. I straighten my shoulders and take a deep breath, then step onto the grass. No alarms blare and no floodlights flash on, so apparently there's no perimeter security. Elena steps up beside me and we walk across the yard and up onto the deck. Elena turns back to check the alley to make sure no one is watching us that she can see. I test the doorknob, which unbelievably is not locked, and the door swings open. Elena hustles inside ahead of me and I quietly close the door. I grip her arm and when she looks at me I put my finger to my lips. She nods her understanding.

We're standing just inside the family room, which looks more like an entertainment center. The lights are off but with the late afternoon sun shining through the windows, we can see everything clearly. We stand still for a few minutes, listening for any indication there is anyone home. The house is completely quiet, but we can't assume it's empty. I gesture for Elena to come closer and speak in a low voice:

"Harry might be hiding, so we'll want to try calling his name to let him know we're here. Before we do that or make any other loud noise, we need to do a walk-through to make sure no one's here."

It takes us only ten minutes or so to check the downstairs rooms, ending up in the front foyer. We climb the stairs to the second floor. There are several closed doors along the hallway and one is standing open, so we check that one first. Once inside, I don't think we realize what we're seeing at first. Elena immediately spots Harry's aquarium and quickly crosses the room to check it.

"He's not in there, but he's got to be somewhere in the house. Do you think he would have tried to come home on his own?"

I don't respond as I walk over to the worktable and finally understand what goes on in this room—and it's not that far off from a mad scientist's lair. I see the mounted insects and make note of the tools of the trade, so to speak. I also don't miss the used cotton ball that's still in Harry's aquarium. The wave of rage I feel actually makes my knees weak, but I have to stay focused. Without calling Elena's attention to all that, I walk out of the room and into the hallway, and stand looking over the railing into the foyer below. Suddenly, I don't care if anyone is here or not. I call out, as loudly as I can. "Harry! Where are you, pal? Can you answer us? Harry!"

Elena comes out to stand beside me. "We'll never find him like this. This house is just too big, and he's so small."

Nevertheless, we both call for him again and again, until

it's clear that it's pointless. I tell Elena that I think our best option is to ask this so-called *Bakari* what they've done with—or to—Harry. Elena grabs her phone from her pocket and starts jabbing buttons. Maybe we can threaten them into cooperating.

"Tristan, I'll bet that was who went in the ambulance when we got here. I'll bet they went to the local hospital. Look, it's only a couple of miles from here. Maybe we could get in to see them."

"Well, we can at least try. Come on, let's get out of here. I guess we'll work out a story on the way to the hospital. We're not relatives and we don't even know their last name." As we walk down the stairs, Elena notices a couple of envelopes lying on a tray sitting on top of an old-fashioned wood hope chest that's pushed up against the back wall of the foyer. She picks up an envelope and shows it to me.

"We do now—this is addressed to Bakari Compline." "Okay then. Let's go pay a charitable visit to this Compline character."

I t's an easy drive to the hospital. One of the benefits of living in a small town such as this one is that the local hospital's emergency department isn't overrun like it would be on a weekend at a big city hospital. Parking is just across the street, which is an even bigger difference. In the city, you'd be lucky to find a parking space within blocks of the hospital. I'm feeling pretty grim; we need to ask this Bakari a few hard questions. We enter the emergency department's exterior sliding door and are immediately stopped before we get to the interior door, which we expected. We have to run through the usual pandemic protocol ("Have you traveled out of the country recently?") and have our temperatures taken by showing our faces to a clever electronic device perched on a pedestal. Once we're through all that and make sure our masks cover our nose and mouth, the receptionist asks what we need to be seen for and Elena steps forward.

"We just found out that a friend was taken ill earlier today and brought here. We're anxious to see them. The name is Bakari Compline."

The receptionist asks for our identifications, which we hand over. She checks the patient list and frowns. "I don't have you on their list of emergency contacts."

I clear my throat. "Well, we wouldn't be, we're not actually family. We have a very close mutual friend by the name of Harry, who wanted us to check on Bakari. Would you be able to let them know that Harry's friends are here and ask if they'll see us?"

The receptionist uses the desk phone to call back to the treatment area. We can't hear what she's saying but she's not frowning when she hangs up.

"Sir, ma'am, you can go on back, Room 3. I'll buzz the door open for you."

We pass through the double doors and into the treatment area, which has a low-level, busy hum of ambient sound. Room 3, immediately to our right, has a glass sliding door that is closed and the view into the room is partially blocked by a privacy curtain. We hesitate and look at each other, then slide the door open and look farther into the room. I assume the person lying on the ER bed is Bakari, who looks to have just awakened and is sitting up. Elena draws in a sharp breath.

"It's just a kid, Tristan. A girl."

I don't care if it's just a toddler, I want some answers. Adults don't have a monopoly on vicious behavior. The kid hears Elena and sits up, but I'm only assuming it's a girl at this point and I'll go with that for now. We enter the room, sliding the door closed behind us. The girl leans back against the pillows, looking puzzled and a little wary.

"The nurse asked me if I wanted visitors and since he mentioned Harry I said it was okay. Who are you guys and how do you know about Harry?"

I abruptly step forward and start to speak, but Elena touches my arm and shakes her head. Okay, so maybe I need to dial down the energy a bit. I step back and gesture for her to go ahead, which is probably a good idea since the girl is starting to look actively concerned instead of wary.

Elena moves to the side of the bed and fiddles with the blanket that covers the girl, gently straightening it out a little. "So, you're Bakari, right?"

The girl nods, but still looks wary. "Yes, I'm Bakari." Her eyes widen and she appears agitated.

"Oh! Oh my God, you must be Harry's *family*! I'm so sorry, if I had known he was an alien and not a rare insect I never would have done it. Is he alright? Where is he?"

Okay, there's a lot to unpack here. I feel a tightening across the back of my head and do some quick breathing exercises in an attempt to ward off the stress headache that's been building up. "Harry's not an alien..."

"*Tristan*, we can get into that later."

Elena turns back to Bakari, who has thrown back the blanket and is trying to get up, but she's still connected to the IV for fluids. She must not have been injured too badly, since she's wearing raggedy jean shorts and T-shirt, and not a hospital gown. She's managed to sit upright, with her legs hanging over the side of the bed, and her bare feet twitch like they'd really like to be on the floor and walking out of here.

"Bakari, we got a message from Harry. We know you took him to your house. We can go into more detail later, but we're trying to find him. That's all. We'd appreciate anything you can do to help us. We're worried he might be hurt."

How Elena can sound so calm is beyond me; she hesitates and looks at me questioningly. I continue the explanation, trying for a calm tone myself. I'm resigned; jail, here we come. I take over the broad explanation.

"Look, we'll be straight with you. We're not here to frighten you or harm you in any way. It's just that we went into your house to look for Harry. We couldn't find him, but we did find your insect lab."

I know my voice sounds very hard but honestly, I don't care. "We were talking to him on his phone, and he went down to the front door to see if it was unlocked. We heard the alarms go off. We're assuming he's still in the house and need you to tell us where we should look for him."

The kid's eyes have gotten very wide. "He was fine when we were talking and—

Wow. I actually stagger; damage control needs to happen right damn now. "What do you mean, when you were talking? Ah—you know Harry's just a bug, right?"

I catch a side glimpse of Elena's raised eyebrow; she seems to be handling this situation much better than I am.

The kid rolls her eyes; yep, teenager here. "Look, I might be young but I'm not *stupid.* You of all people should understand that Harry's not *just a bug.*"

She has the nerve to do air quotes at me, and with attitude no less. "Harry and I had a rough start, okay, which was *totally* my fault and I'll own that, but we were making up. He was talking to me and the next thing I know, I wake up here. I have no idea what happened between then and now."

Just then a tired-looking doctor bustles into the room. She looks at Bakari and then us. "Are you this young lady's parents?"

Bakari waves her non-IV'ed hand toward us by way of introduction. "No, these are my friends Tristan and Elena.

My parents are out of town, and they're here to give me a ride home when I'm discharged."

I kind of choke at such a blatant lie, and Elena surreptitiously elbows me, accompanied by a little side-eye glare. The doctor doesn't notice this sideshow. She takes a moment to read some chart notes and pulls up a stool beside the bed, then starts going over test results with Bakari, glancing up occasionally to include us in the discussion.

"All your tests came back normal, no indication of anything that would have caused you to pass out. Since there are no issues that we can find at this time, I don't see a need to admit you for further observation. We don't know why you passed out at home, but you seem to be fine now. You don't appear to have bumped your head so we're ruling out a concussion, but you should still take it easy for a day or so. Any dizziness at all?"

Bakari shakes her head. "No, I feel pretty good now, actually."

The doctor nods. "Well, since your parents aren't here and you're 16, you can sign your own discharge paperwork. I'll send the nurse in with that and aftercare instructions. Be sure to let us know right away if things change."

Bakari nods her understanding, and the doctor pats her hand and hurries out the door. Even though this emergency department isn't overrun, it's still pretty busy. The three of us look at each other, not saying anything. I sit down on the stool the doctor was using and Elena takes the bedside chair. Bakari starts to say something just as the nurse bustles in. He quickly disconnects the IV line from the back of Bakari's hand and generally tidies things up.

"You're all cleared for release." He smiles kindly at her. "I'm sure you have better things to do than hang around here." He hands her a clipboard holding several pages of forms. "Sign at all the places marked with an X, please. After- care instructions are all here. Get plenty of rest over the next couple of days and let us know if you start feeling worse."

Bakari hands the clipboard back to the nurse, who detaches several pages and hands them back to her. He bustles back out of the room, talking over his shoulder to us as he exits.

"I'll be right back with a wheelchair and we'll get you folks on your way."

This has all happened fast and now we're committed, with no chance for second thoughts. The last thing I had planned for today was to take custody of a teenaged delinquent. Elena gazes at Bakari for a moment, then shakes her head in resignation.

"Tristan, why don't you go get the car and meet us outside the emergency entrance where we came in. I'll walk out with Bakari. We can all talk in the car."

It's a few minutes of bustle later to get everyone settled in the car, and we head out of the parking lot. The plan to talk in the car was a good one, but after several minutes of travel no one is saying anything. As I pull onto the highway, Elena shifts around so she can see Bakari, who is belted into the back seat.

"We're glad you're okay. We need to find Harry and we're hoping you can help us."

Bakari doesn't seem to be intimidated by Elena, and nods in agreement. "I'll definitely help you look everywhere. I sure hope he's okay."

Elena gives her a surprisingly hard look. "I don't want to upset you, but he's in this situation because of your actions. Regardless, we need to set that aside and focus on finding him. We were talking to Harry when we heard an alarm go off. When we got to your house, police, fire, and the ambulance were in the process of leaving. Do you have any idea what happened right before all that?"

I look at Bakari in the rearview mirror. "We're not trying to threaten you, and like I said we're certainly not going to harm you in any way whatsoever. You don't know us and have no reason to trust us, but we hope you will. You need to understand this is very serious. Harry's welfare is at stake and we think you'd like to help him."

She looks down at her hands, gripped tightly in her lap. "I understand. Harry is very special. Let me think a minute." She closes her eyes and leans her head on the back of her seat. She looks tired, and I belatedly remember that she went to the hospital for a reason. Bakari sighs and opens her eyes, leaning forward to speak more directly to Elena.

"I was out for all of that commotion. The only thing I can think of is that Harry must have somehow tried to unlock the front door using the security keypad. The last time I did that, I got a little static shock when I pushed the disarm button. I told my dad about it and he was going to call an electrician, but then he had to go out of town with my mom. I've been using an app on my phone to set and disarm the alarm, not the keypad."

I consider this, imagining the scene. "Was the keypad disarm button maybe a little sticky, so that you would have had to press it more firmly?"

Bakari looks at me in surprise. "Yeah, how did you know?"

"I think I know what happened. Harry has this special little talent, where he can add a little extra energy to an action so that it has more force. I expect the force he applied combined with whatever was causing that static spark, and he probably got shocked. Depending on the strength of the shock, he could have been flung across the room and knocked out. In that case, he'd have to still be in that room, in the foyer somewhere."

Elena turns to face the windshield and is clearly frustrated and upset. "But where could he be? We looked everywhere in that area."

Bakari clears her throat. "Could he have been thrown back kind of in a straight line from the front door?"

I envision the event and nod. "Probably. The foyer area isn't that large, so if the combined electrical discharge was great enough he could easily have been thrown up against the opposite wall."

She grabs the back of my seat in excitement. "So if he hit the wall, he would have slid down it to the floor."

Elena and I look at each other and say at the same time, "He's still under that hope chest."

CHAPTER THREE

We don't waste any time getting back to Bakari's house and soon we're parked in her driveway. We rapidly exit the car and hurry up the walk to the front door. Bakari trails a little way behind and seems to be feeling the effects of whatever caused her to be taken to the hospital. I turn back to her and offer a steadying hand on her elbow, which she hesitantly accepts. Surprisingly, the door isn't locked, so we enter and stand together a little awkwardly in the small foyer.

A plain-looking hope chest, made of dark wood with a subdued finish, is standing up against the wall directly in front of us. Some styles of this type of furniture sit flat on the floor, but this one has wedge-shaped feet that lift it up an inch or so. Elena immediately kneels in front of it, shines her cudgel/flashlight back and forth underneath it, then sits back on her heels with a frustrated sigh.

"I checked this when we were here before, but he has to be under here." She jumps up and hands the flashlight to Bakari. "I still can't see him. We need to lift this up out of the way."

Bakari moves aside. Elena and I each grab an end of the chest and very carefully lift it, take a couple of steps back, then set it down in the middle of the foyer floor. We can see Harry lying with his back to us, scrunched up against the wall. He's not moving and I try not to assume the worst. Bakari moves toward Harry but Elena touches her arm to hold her back.

"Let Tristan check him first."

I think she doesn't want to be the one to discover he's not with us any longer, but I have to see what I can do. I take a knee beside him, bending down to get close enough that I can see he's breathing. I don't see any obvious signs of injury, so maybe he did just get knocked out by the electric shock. Unfortunately, I have no idea how to check him for a concussion. I very gently touch his back and softly call his name. He twitches a little, which is encouraging. I bump him a tiny bit harder to see if I can get him to move again, but he's really out. I sit back on my heels to think this through. Now that we've found him, I'm no longer running on an adrenaline rush, and I'm wiped out, physically and emotionally. I can see dark circles under Elena's eyes and know she's in the same state. I'm wondering the best way to pick him up when Bakari clears her throat and steps closer.

"I could bring his aquarium down here, so you could get him comfortable in there and not have to worry about carrying him around."

Elena nods at her. "That's a good idea. I'll walk up there with you."

They slowly start up the stairs, Bakari gripping the banister with her right hand while Elena supports her left elbow. I had thought Elena was going with the kid to make sure she doesn't do anything crazy, but I realize Elena is reacting to Bakari's young age and is in care-mode. I don't know Bakari, of course, but I think she doesn't look too good and I'm sure Elena sees that more clearly than I do. I guess any blame and recrimina-tion conversation with Bakari will have to wait. At this rate we probably won't have one, but I don't see the kid getting away without at least a tough lecture. And just where the hell *are* her parents? I don't believe the business trip story and can't wait to hear the real one.

I can hear footsteps overhead and voices murmuring. I wonder if Bakari is trying to explain the whole mad-scientist set up but their voices sound pretty calm, so probably not. I hope Elena is focused on retrieving the aquarium and not thinking about what went on in that room. They finally come back down, Elena holding the aquarium and Bakari carrying what looks like a miniature toolbox. I guess that's the best we can do for now, unless she's come up with the name of a bug vet. Elena kneels opposite me and places the aquarium on the floor beside her. I see that Harry's phone is still adhered to the glass at one end, with the charging cord bundled up under it. I take the cord and stuff it in my jacket pocket. Elena smooths out the aquarium bedding a little and looks over at Harry, then back at me, so I guess I'm the designated mantis-EMT for now.

Harry is lying in an odd position, facing the wall, and I don't know the best way to approach trying to move him. Bakari sits cross-legged on the floor and places her toolbox in her lap. When she opens it, I can see the tools of what I now consider a murderous occupation. She lays out several items: a blank 3x5 index card, a long swab, and a small vial labeled alcohol. There are a number of other items in the box, but I decide not to think about their purposes. Bakari looks at me with a guilty expression. My eyebrows clench in agreement. I must have looked intimidating, as she flinches a bit. Elena glares at me but I shrug and get to the point.

"Well, here we are. Whatever issues we may with each

other, our first priority is helping Harry. Anyone with an idea, just throw it out there."

Bakari clears her throat and looks at her hands, which are shaking a bit, as she starts talking.

"I know this is all my fault, but I think I can help. Here's what I think we should do. First, we need to get him off the floor and into his aquarium. Then we have to see about waking him up."

When I hear "waking him up," my heart leaps like it's taken its own static shock. I realize something I hadn't even thought of until now—what if Harry's gone into stasis? Too many terrible thoughts hit my brain at the same time. If we can't wake him up, what do we do, bury him somewhere and hope he comes back again? I could never be sure a place we could choose would be safe for him for years, let alone decades or centuries. If we were to do something so monstrous, what if he actually is just in a deep, healing sleep? I think I start to hyperventilate, but Elena grabs my arm and shakes it.

"Tristan, focus. We can only do our best and take a step at a time. You know this. We have to have faith that we can help him."

As always, she's right. We have to focus on the moment in front of us; the future will turn out as it will. It's hard to see past my own distress, but there are tears on Bakari's face again and my bad feelings toward her loosen up a little. I sigh and relax my cramped posture and hope I can deal with whatever the future hands out. I give Bakari a look with a little less sizzle in it.

"Okay, let's see what we can do. Bakari, you have something in mind?"

The girl hastily wipes her cheeks with one hand and hands me the index card with the other.

"I thought, well, that we need to keep his body stable while lifting him, so I don't think we should try picking him up with just our hands. We need something stiff enough to support him but thin enough to slide under him to pick him up. This is the only thing I could think of that might work."

I think that's actually a good idea. I take the index card and inspect its edge, then hold my breath as I place it at his back and gently start wiggling it, slowing sliding it under him as I move the card forward. Harry's limp body moves easily onto the card. Once he's aboard, I very carefully move him to the aquarium. Elena has made a little bed-type arrangement in the middle of the aquarium and I tilt the card slightly to deposit him on it. I let my breath go and slowly move the card back and away. I realize a large part of the stress I'm feeling is alleviated simply by getting him off the floor. It feels like we're getting some control of the situation. I look back to Bakari for the next step, waking him up. I see she's putting the cotton tip of the swab into the vial holding the alcohol.

"You're going to try holding that under his nose, right? Don't we need, what is it, smelling salts instead? Like the little capsules you see medics use in the movies?"

She nods. "Yes, that would make sense, but I didn't have anything like that. I thought we could try seeing if alcohol would work."

Elena agrees. "I don't think it will hurt him if we're careful. Here, let me try it."

Bakari hands her the swab. Elena sits on the floor and scoots closer to the aquarium. She carefully extends the swab and wafts it back and forth in front of Harry's face, using very small movements. Harry twists his head away; we all gasp excitedly. Elena moves the swab a little more broadly, and we can all see Harry open his eyes. We hold our breath as we watch him shakily sit up. He briefly clutches his head between both mittens, then leans back and props himself up on his elbows. He looks up at us hovering anxiously over the aquarium, and I have a random thought that our faces must look huge to him from this angle. He tries to speak but is probably dehydrated. He clears his throat and tries again.

"What the hell hit me? I think I saw dead people."

The relief is nearly overwhelming, and we three humans laugh. Harry is understandably puzzled and not at all amused. I try to get myself under control.

"Hey, pal, we're just really glad to see you. This might be a really stupid question, all things considered, but are you okay?"

Harry takes a minute to consider this. He rubs his head, then checks out his arms and all his legs. It looks to me like he's moving all right, maybe just a little stiffly. He stands up from his bed analog and doesn't wobble too much. Those spindly limbs are deceptive; he's tougher than he looks.

"Well, I feel like I've been run over by something several magnitudes larger and heavier than myself, but everything appears to be operational. Other than this headache, I don't seem to be in pain. I don't think I'll try flying just yet, though. That last landing was a doozy. I feel like I could sleep for years."

He sees my appalled expression and quickly backtracks, waving his arms at us. "No, I didn't mean stasis! I just meant I could use a good night's sleep. Or two. That's all."

Bakari timidly raises a hand to interrupt. "What do you mean, stasis?"

Harry doesn't answer the stasis question and scowls at her instead. "You're finally awake, I see."

She nods and looks pretty miserable, so much so that I find myself feeling a little sorry for her. Just a little, though; personally, I think it's way too early to let her off the hook. Elena pats her hand sympathetically. More of that care-mode stuff that doesn't seem to come naturally to me. Harry appears to relent as well and tiredly waves it off with his mitten as he continues.

"The telling of this story could take days, if not weeks. I wasn't kidding when I said I saw dead people. Remind me to tell you about the ship. I've had enough adventure to last me the next couple of lifetimes together, and the only thing I want now is to go home."

Going home sounds like a fantastic idea, but we have unfinished business with Bakari.

PART SIX

EARLY AUTUMN IN THE YEAR OF OUR
LORD, 1565

The 600-ton galleon traveled the Atlantic Ocean currents under full sail, hypnotically rising and falling with the waves under a full moon in a now-clear sky. She was a proud vessel of the Spanish Treasure Fleet, now serving as the flagship of this special purpose fleet. She was accompanied on this voyage by a number of somewhat smaller sister ships having lesser tonnage. This fleet collectively carried not just its regular crew of some ten score sailors and military complement of several hundred soldiers, but also several score of colonists—men, women, and children, along with several priests. Various of the colonists, as well as some of the soldiers, were skilled craftsman that were crucial for establishing and maintaining the new colony: there were builders, blacksmiths, tanners, armorers, clothiers, cobblers and more; perhaps considered the most critical of such skills were those of the farmers and brewery masters. All were bound for *La Florida* under the orders of King Philip II of Spain. The new settlement would further secure Spain's claim to territory in the New World and hold France's colonizing efforts there at bay. Everyone, on all the ships of the fleet and regardless of their station or skill, intended to take whatever fortune they could wrest from this venture.

The voyage thus far had been no more fraught with worry and danger than was usual for a voyage that typically spanned nearly three months. For this night at least the weather was calm, as the most recent thunderstorm had passed several hours ago. The ship's sails were rigged to capture the full strength of the air currents flowing above the triple masts as surely as its hull clung to the watery currents below the keel. The ship's navigator charted the ship's heading to follow both currents, which he had come to know as well as he knew the breezes and contours of his homeland. The night watchman handling the rudder at the stern was alert at his station, although it was the deepest part of the night. The only sounds that could be heard were the occasional slap of a sail and the constant hissing sound of the waves sliding along the keel. The ship's human cargo was much more active during daylight hours, with sailors rushing about on deck carrying out the many tasks that kept the ship afloat, soldiers maintaining weapons and skills, and colonists lining the deck railings seeking in the sea breezes a temporary relief from the harsh shipboard conditions. Now, the colonists slept, if they could, in their assigned belowdecks compartments while soldiers and sailors slept wherever they could find a space to hang a hammock or throw down a sleeping mat.

Stalker was also a passenger aboard the flagship. His presence was unintentional, the result of having made his most recent stasis den in what turned out to be an insecure location. It had happened that after several months of footsore traveling, his previous companions, Brother Alwin and Brother Eustace, had chosen to end their journey eastward upon reaching a small coastal village. The village faced the sea, located at a trading point that had gone dormant during the Great Pestilence. The brothers agreed that further travel would be postponed, and so petitioned the villagers to make a permanent home there. They would reopen the village's church and hold services, and minister to their small congregation. The village had lost nearly all its residents, along with its priest, to the Great Pestilence but was slowly recovering. The two monks were made welcome with much gratitude.

Like his companions, Stalker was ready to cease traveling for a time. He had never made himself known to the two monks, or to any other human, during this time of his life. After the emotional trauma of his own losses caused by the plague, he was reluctant to foster the type of loving friendship he'd had with Brother Mark. It was a deep comfort for him just to be near enough other living beings to eavesdrop on their lives from his various hiding places. He became part of the village shadows but was content and went about rebuilding his own quiet life in this new location. There were innumerable new things to observe, and there were even different animals from which to escape. Unfortunately, this new location had both crows and cats. It seemed that these difficult beings would always inhabit any place in which he found himself. Despite the inherent dangers involved in moving about the countryside, Stalker became adept at finding ways to join travelers heading to places he wanted to explore.

Stalker had lived a peaceful life in the village for nearly two centuries before he felt the need for a stasis period begin to rise. He was puzzled that the compulsion to sleep was stirring, since he hadn't sustained any significant injury that would have needed a long-term repair. He thought it might possibly have to do with his accumulated time in this body.

Lately he often found himself with virtually no energy, and his movements were no longer quick and spritely. It was taking longer and longer for his energy to restore, and his energy reserves would barely increase despite the longer basking times. Regardless of the cause, he must sleep and to do so he needed to find a safe place. He soon found a group of villagers who were preparing to go hunting medicinal herbs in the forest and had hidden himself in the bottom of a collection basket. While he was carried to the forest thusly, he made his plan to find the perfect den location.

His ideal outcome would be to find a burrow that had already been dug and then abandoned by its original owner, where he could excavate a tiny den at the very end and tuck himself in for a long rest period. He had always liked a good, deep burrow for sleeping through stasis. Finding a place that would remain undisturbed for possibly centuries had become more difficult as humanity continued to expand into the broader world, but Stalker believed he'd be able to find such a burrow somewhere beneath the broad root systems of the pine trees in this forest. When the village girl placed her basket on the ground and started looking for herbs, Stalker quickly scrambled out of it and scurried away into the forest brush.

It took him a few days to explore more deeply into the forest, away from the paths that led to the village, looking for the perfect burrow beneath the roots of the perfect tree. He entertained pleasantly high hopes while he browsed the various berry bushes as he wandered. He even tried some of the edible herbs the villagers were hunting, but they made a bitter meal. Stalker knew better than to try certain of the fungi; he felt his life was surreal enough without outside assistance. Stalker finally spotted a mature pine tree that had looked perfect to him. As he suspected, there was indeed an abandoned burrow that would suit his needs, and it wasn't long before he was tightly curled up in a den at the end of it. He was safe and comfortable, and passed through the initial slowing of his body's processes to enter the final stasis phase where his body would be repaired, and possibly reconfigured, during a period that could last for thousands of years.

Unfortunately, such a lengthy stasis period was not to be had this time. Scarcely two score years after Stalker curled up in his den, the tree covering his burrow was again found to be perfect, this time for the needs of traders who wished to export timber for shipbuilding. The tall, straight pine trees in the forests surrounding the coastal village were well-suited for use as ship masts and had come to be in great demand. The tree covering Stalker's burrow was destined for a far different use.

The all-consuming noise and earth-shaking caused by the logging process forced Stalker from deep stasis into consciousness. His den was collapsing around him. Now thoroughly awake, he scrambled, dug, and clawed his way into the open. He saw the formerly mighty tree being reduced to nothing more than a rough pine log. He also saw the large group of woodsmen stamping about and knew he had to find safety away from all those feet. He huddled low to the flattened soil above his former den as the trunk was trimmed, then trussed in ropes for oxen to pull out of the forest, and eventually to the shipping port. When the trunk was pulled away from the remaining stump, the movement dislodged dusty material that had covered the opening of an insect borehole. Stalker saw a chance of concealment and scurried for the opening. He squeezed himself inside and wriggled farther up into the trunk, all the way to the end of the borehole.

While the borehole was narrow and extended into the trunk for only a few inches, the small space was sufficient for his immediate purposes. Feeling secure for the moment, Stalker let himself relax. However, relaxation soon led to sleep, and sleep led to an unintended return to stasis. So it was that in time, Stalker would become an inadvertent sailor, and would eventually become an inadvertent colonist.

It is the nature of shipbuilding that shipwrights must use seasoned wood. After a short sea voyage to its export destination, the log in which Stalker was peacefully secured spent its required time, undisturbed, in a seasoning shed. Eventually the shipwrights determined the log was ready for use, and it was again roped to oxen for transport, this time to the shipyard. Stalker slept through the movement of this transport, and he slept through the swinging movement of the log as a dock crane lifted it into position above the deck of the nearly complete ship. Stalker did not sleep through the abrupt, heavy jolt when the log was roughly dropped to settle onto the deck. He awoke greatly confused, but his innate safety protocols were also awakened and prodded him to brace himself in the borehole. He held himself steady in the narrow space, legs quivering, as the log was hauled upright for placement as the ship's third, rear-most mast. He remained in the borehole, even as workers quickly slathered the now-mast from top to bottom with tarry pitch, sealing the borehole opening below Stalker with a thin layer of the stuff.

Eventually day turned to night and the work crews left the ship, leaving several guards placed here and there. Randomly placed torches lit the deck. Stalker found that the tiny claws at the ends of his forelegs worked very well to scrape aside the pitch, and he could soon see through the small hole he had made. He was astounded at the strange scene before his eyes, so different from anything he remembered having experienced before. He didn't remember ever seeing a ship, much less an ocean; this was all utterly new to him. Worryingly, there was nothing resembling food in sight, but there was an open barrel of water nearby. That would have to do for now. The flickering shadows thrown by the torches aided him in traversing the short section of deck from the mast to the barrel, and he soon had his fill of clean water. He heard a loud noise and scrambled back to his borehole. He decided he would continue to reside in the borehole while he explored this new environment.

The days passed, and the ship was launched. The borehole became uncomfortable and Stalker longed to stretch his legs. After several terrifyingly close escapes early in the voyage, Stalker had finally found a hidden space under a deck railing where he could remain hidden until it was dark enough for him to be nearly invisible against the damp wood of the open deck. Even then, he must remain vigilant; movement in the dark could also capture the attention of a human eye. The humans on the ship, while superficially pious in their religion, were generally a crude and unhappy group, and Stalker had learned he could not safely be seen by them. Stalker wasn't nocturnal by nature, but he necessarily had only the dark of night for foraging for whatever sustenance he could find. After nearly three months into the journey, food had become scarce for all the beings on the ship, and even crumbs were rare. He had been forced into taking longer and longer sleep periods to conserve energy, until he became concerned that he would lapse into stasis from starvation and thirst. There was no safe place onboard this ship he could trust to remain undisturbed during stasis.

Extreme discomfort wasn't for only the humans to suffer. The continual spray of ocean mist left his normally silky hair stiff and salt-encrusted, and he had quickly learned that ingesting too much salt while grooming left him feeling very ill. He was limited to performing minimal grooming, just enough to retain some semblance of flexibility in his legs. Despite his suffering, he didn't regret having become a colonist himself, although in retrospect he admitted to himself that he would have done a better job of planning for this voyage, given the opportunity. He didn't know what he could have changed, though; it wasn't like he could have brought his own supplies.

For now, Stalker resigned himself to another night of moon-gazing instead of foraging. The full moon's light shone too brightly on deck to facilitate stealthy movement, and after all, he had had a few crumbs just the day before. He could last until tomorrow, but he'd definitely have to find food then. His energy was dangerously low. He sighed and decided that for this night, he would try venturing out of hiding just a bit farther, in order to obtain a better view of the full moon. During his time at the monastery, he had been able to learn the basic elements of astronomy, which were enough to help him identify constellations and chart his own course through time in concert with the phases of the moon. He had listened to the sailors talking and knew they were nearing their destination; he just needed to persevere for a few days longer, surely he could manage that.

Stalker leaped to the deck as the ship tilted upward, rising on a wave. He stood motionless in a convenient shadow until he was satisfied there was nothing immediately threatening to his well-being. He ran several Stalker-paces across the deck to a stack of looped rigging rope that stood a third of a meter high and was half of that wide. The rope loops were bound on the sides by thinner rope to hold the stack together, and the whole stack was tied securely by yet more rope that was knotted around specialized cleats pounded into the deck. Stalker hurriedly climbed down into the open coils, then peeked out over the top loop. He was relieved that there were no humans to be seen. He slowly and cautiously moved farther out along the top of the coiled rope, luxuriating in his solitude and momentary safety.

His view of the moonlit sky was unobstructed, and the

cloud-free expanse of star-spanned heavens took his breath away. In that moment, he finally understood his need to travel, to see, to experience and learn new things. He had thought, until then, that it was his curiosity that drove him to constantly question, to constantly desire new information. Now he understood that his sometimes overwhelming curiosity was merely the trigger that motivated him to take actions that would fulfill this underlying need. He knew then that no matter how long he might live, he would always continue to travel; he would learn, and he vowed that before the end of his traveling, he would understand who and what he was. If he had a purpose, he vowed he would understand that, too.

From the corner of his eye, he glimpsed an odd shimmer of movement, and he was distracted from his musings to more clearly focus his attention on this phenomenon. At first he thought it was what Brother Mark had called a "shooting star," but instead of a point of light arcing across the sky to disappear beyond the horizon, this vertical light appeared to have two distinct ends. It appeared as a slightly wavy line about three meters in length, extremely thin but still having a discernable width. The top end of the line hung unsupported, its overall glow eclipsing that of the stars behind it, and its ending point appeared to touch the water. In his objective mind, Stalker thought it was odd that the water didn't boil and steam since to him the line looked like a short piece of stretched-out lightning. The line advanced forward in a measured manner toward the ship. In his subjective mind, his increasing panic made it hard to breathe properly.

It was impossible that none of the ship's crew had seen this display. He expected to hear alarms at any moment, but his hearing was curiously muffled. The night watchman sounded no alarm. There were no human voices shouting in fear, and no one raced up from belowdecks to fight off boarders. The sound of wind and wave was likewise muted, and equally impossibly, even the surging movement of the ship appeared to have slowed to the speed of a human's walking pace. His expectation of calamity increased, but there was nothing he could do other than creep back into the shadows of the coiled rope and continue watching potential disaster unfold.

As Stalker sat shivering in fear of the unknown, he saw the bottom end of the vertical line come to rest on the deck near the rear-most of the three masts, quite near his hiding place. This situation was not necessarily what he would consider a learning experience, but as usual, his curiosity was beginning to overtake the fear. The line began to broaden, until it became recognizably like a doorway, then a foot stepped forward from inside the glowing doorway. The foot was attached to the leg of a bipedally-shaped figure, which proceeded to fully step across the doorway's threshold. The figure stood erect with both feet firmly set on the non- moving deck, at which point the line of light silently disappeared behind it. Stalker felt a little lightheaded when the glow abruptly vanished and he could see the moon- washed deck again. His night vision had been wrecked, but once the glow-engendered violet and green spots had faded from his eyesight, he could see that the figure wasn't just bipedal; it appeared to be a mature human woman.

Although the figure looked feminine to Stalker it was oddly dressed like a man, and not just any sort of man but recognizably like an English privateer. As English privateers were the particular bane of the Spanish Treasure Fleet, Stalker thought it was pretty nervy of the figure to be dressed like that since she was standing on the deck of a Spanish galleon. He had the momentary, dizzying thought that although there was an absence of visible weapons, perhaps this person believed they would commandeer the ship singlehandedly. This was worrisome; during his sea voyage Stalker had overheard the crew tell tales of privateer raids, and of the many resulting ghostly shipwrecks lurking in the depths below, huddled over their lost treasure.

The woman, for a woman it was, turned in a full circle, taking in a deep breath of sea air as she did so. Her thick, dark hair, uncovered and shadowed with gray, hung to her shoulders in a multitude of beaded plaits, which stood out from her broad shoulders as she turned. She flung both arms out wide, threw back her head and laughed quietly, and stamped a booted foot on the deck as if to check its solidity. Her slightly tilted eyes glistened and the smooth, mahogany- dark skin of her face shone with health. Along with the boots she wore a loose, thin white shirt with flowing sleeves, a leather jerkin, and breeches of a heavy, thick cloth. She was slender in body and much taller than the women, and most of the men, that Stalker was used to seeing in this time. Her hands looked strong and capable. She glanced down and spotted Stalker sitting just inside the top of the rope coil. She spoke aloud, with a trace of the warm melody and rhythm of the crew's language in her voice.

"Finally! There you are, my little wanderer. I've had quite the fine time catching up with you. Come out, come out. You should know there is no harm to come from me."

The woman's voice was low and pleasant, and her eyes seemed to sparkle with the missing light from the occluded stars. Stalker didn't trust her at all and took a slow step backward.

"Now, now, none of that!" She stepped forward and Stalker felt the coarse surface of the rope fall away from his feet as she carefully picked him up. After a wild, futile scrabbling with his legs, he let them droop limply as he was placed on the palm of the woman's other hand. There was nowhere to run and the deck seemed a long way down. The woman didn't have the stature of a giant, but still, she was immensely larger than himself. He'd been in many strange and questionable circumstances, but this situation was taking pride of place at the top of his weirdness list. The woman gently stroked his back while making a shushing sound and Stalker braced himself, ready to mount a defense if at all possible.

"None of that, either. Here, let's get comfortable, the two of us, and have a little visit. I've come a long way to find you, in this time and in this place."

The thought of being sought out by such an entity didn't fill Stalker with comfort. The woman settled onto the deck and leaned back against the rope coil where Stalker had been hiding. She sat comfortably cross-legged and placed Stalker on her right knee. He thought about jumping down and running from there, but instead tried using mind-speak to protest being hoisted aloft. He reached out to the woman's mind in his usual manner but encountered what seemed to be a dense, gray fog that blocked his attempt. When he didn't respond aloud, the woman leaned in close to him and gave him a disconcertingly intense look.

"I felt you reach out just then, but for now you'll need to actually verbalize—ah, I see—it's the memory problem. Well, we can't have that, can we? Here, let's try this."

She extended her right index finger and touched Stalker's forehead, right between his eyes, so softly that he barely felt it. What he did feel was a tiny jolt of energy that caused every hair on his small body to stand straight out from his skin and begin to vibrate. The vibrations nearly caused him to slip sideways off the woman's knee, but she steadied him with her hand, watching him closely. The vibrations weren't painful, but they were extremely intense; Stalker closed his eyes and shouted with anxiety. Then he stopped, opened his eyes, and shouted again, but this time he realized he could hear himself through his own ears. The hair on his body relaxed. This was definitely new territory for this current lifetime, but at the same time he knew it wasn't new to himself; he could remember being *able* to speak, but not when or how. He drew in a great breath, had a stunned, joyful thought, and felt the hair on his body rise in tandem with it.

"*Hallelujah! I can speak aloud!*"

The woman laughed loudly and shook her head. "Well, I wouldn't have thought your very first word after so long would have been hallelujah, but I guess that's what a few hundred years living with monks will do for a person."

Stalker didn't stop to wonder how she knew about his time in the monastery. He felt like he could fly if he tried. He carefully capered in place on the woman's knee; there were so many words in his mind jostling to be noticed that he couldn't get his brain to settle on any one of them. He was, oddly, speechless.

"*Wait—how ... who...*" He stuttered to a frustrated halt.

The woman gazed at him sympathetically, and, Stalker thought, a little sadly. "I know, it's somewhat of a step down from being able to communicate mind to mind. But this will serve when there's no mind about that can be trusted."

Stalker was having spots in front of his eyes again and it occurred to him that he really should breathe. He forced himself to curl up into a crouch atop the knee, his legs tucked under his body, much like a cat would do. He closed his eyes and without conscious thought a meditative, prayerful chant came into his mind. He relaxed into the beauty and rhythm of the words and felt a deep calmness spread throughout his being. When he opened his eyes, he thought the woman still looked sad, but she was smiling.

"Let's slow things down a little and give you time to catch up. I know your memory has been severely compromised, but we'll just have to work around that. First, let me re-introduce myself. My name is Ngendo, which means 'traveler' in Swahili, the main language my Kenyan parents spoke. I expect you have no idea what Swahili and Kenyan mean. Fun fact, my name is spelled *N-g-e-n-d-o* but pronounced *Jendo.* Anyway, this isn't the first time we've met, not by far. You and I are actually very good friends, but I know you can't remember that yet."

He looked at the woman, truly seeing her for the first time

without the obscuring haze of paralyzing fear. A shadow did cross his mind; she was not completely unfamiliar. The memories of how and when they knew each other were lost to him, but a dim *feeling* of her remained. Unfortunately, that dim feeling wasn't sufficient for him to automatically trust her now, or anything she said. Ngendo was watching him closely. "Yes, I can see you do remember me a little. Well, the

rest will come to you, and I'll just have to be patient in the meantime."

Stalker tried out his newly recovered communication skill, which came more easily, word by word. He was still a little frightened, but that fear was being overtaken, and he was beginning to feel miffed. This person was being controlling and presumptuous, which were not character traits he held in high regard.

"*You claim that we are friends, yet I have no true recollection of you. If you had appeared thus at the monastery, the brothers would name you a demon. I have never seen a demon and I don't believe they exist on this Earth, but I have often saw humans carry out what I felt were demonic acts. You appear to have made time stand still, so I must deduct that you can manipulate time to facilitate your purposes. Perhaps these are demonic acts you are performing with the intent to cause harm.*"

Ngendo grinned broadly. She shifted her seated position so that her back rested against the coiled stack of rope, making sure not to jostle Stalker from his perch on her knee.

"That was quite a long speech for someone who learned to talk just mere seconds ago. I wonder where all those words have been hiding."

Stalker's miffed state ascended to being nearly annoyed. He uncurled himself and peevishly raised a foreleg to point at her. "*I do not wish to participate in your levity. How do I know you do not plan to sink this ship? Why are you here?*"

"Calm down, I'm just teasing you, but I can tell you aren't in the mood for it."

Stalker crossed his forelegs in front of him, which put them right under his chin; if he'd had the right balance he would have been tapping a couple of feet as well. Ngendo sighed and pushed her braids behind an ear, the bangles on her wrists chiming pleasantly with her movement. She had hoped, unrealistically, that her friend would remember at least a little of their times together. Although she knew what he had been through, she hadn't realized the full extent of the psychic and physical damage Stalker had experienced at the hands of the shaman. He was a very different person now, and there was no guarantee that her old friend would ever return. She refused to give in to that despairing thought and continued in an abashed tone.

"Okay, sorry, I'll be serious. There will be no ship- sinking, at least that is caused by me. My only reason for being here is to visit you. We lost track of each other, and I was just recently able to determine your whereabouts. Of the two of us you were always the one to think and speak *very* precisely. I'll try to make sense of this situation for you, such as I can."

Stalker knew he had no real choice other than to take her statements at face value. However bizarre the current situation might be it seemed there was no immediate danger, and certainly if there was, he had no power to either stop it or mitigate it. Accepting this, he returned to his more comfortable cat-crouch on her knee. With a foreleg he performed the universally recognized gesture for Ngendo to continue speaking.

"Do you want to start with any specific questions? Now that you know I don't intend to sink the ship?"

Stalker sighed in his turn. "*I have no idea what to ask, at least what to ask first. Excepting all the questions about how and why you are here, the most obvious is how have you made it so that I can speak aloud? Are you unable to participate in mind-shouting?"*

Ngendo nodded and struggled to hold back a smile. "*Mind-shouting*, right. We used to call it telepathy, and I'm not sure why it isn't working between us at the moment. The two of us used it when we wanted to communicate privately if others were around. The interference now could be anything from the emotions we're experiencing to differing energy levels. I'd have to do some research to answer the question properly. However, your other questions are a good starting place to explain things. In order to understand the verbal communication process, there is a vast amount of underlying data."

Stalker politely waved to interrupt her. "*What is this data?"*

She shook her head ruefully. "I forgot just how much catching up we have to do. Data is simply information, in any form. Because of the damage caused by the way you ended up in this bodily configuration, you aren't able to access your stored information..."

She stopped again upon seeing Stalker's very blank expression and gritted her teeth. "If only causality would have let me get my hands on that shaman—but never mind about that. I think what I'll do now is try for a very basic explanation about our communication skills. We'll go through it a step at a time. How does that sound?"

Stalker was relieved. For all the understanding he had of Ngendo's words she might have been speaking an utterly foreign language, despite sounding like the common language he had heard spoken daily during his time at the monastery. Stalker had easily come to understand the shipboard language, which was different from the monks' common language, which itself was different from that used by the brothers during their religious services. The words he was hearing

Ngendo speak now were difficult for him to grasp; they seemed so familiar yet were somehow crisper and fresher.

"That would be very helpful, thank you. But first, you say you know me, yet you have not mentioned my name. I assume you already know this, but I am called Stalker." In spite of himself he felt the smallest spark of hope rise in the back of his mind. *"Do you by chance know me by that name?"*

Ngendo lifted an eyebrow. "I think the better question is whether Stalker is a name by which you know yourself. What I mean is, do you think it suits you? If you had a choice, would you call yourself something different?" She seemed to wait expectantly, hopefully, as if this were what the brothers would have a called a "significant event."

Her questions surprised Stalker. He hadn't thought of a name as other than something someone else had settled upon him, based upon that person's own perceptions and expectations of Stalker. This was a tasty new idea; if he were able to choose, what *would* he call himself?

"If I had the power to choose, I think I would like to call myself Harry. Given the general hairiness of this body it feels right and is a small but entertaining jest. The name does have a noble history, you know. There have been several kings of my home country who were named Henry, and who were also called Harry."

Ngendo did a triumphant fist-pump in the air, something Stalker had not seen done before. He liked it and wondered briefly how one did it with eight legs. Ngendo grinned broadly, bright teeth shining in her dark face, green eyes glowing with delight.

"Yes! You *absolutely* have that power, and Harry you will be called forthwith. I think it suits you very well, and the jest is indeed entertaining."

CHAPTER THREE

Stalker, newly self-christened Harry, was bewildered by Ngendo's enthusiasm, but there were more important things on his mind just then. *"If you would, please explain how it is I can communicate aloud? Seeing as how I have no vocal organs in this body?"*

She nodded her head, but her clenched eyebrows indicated some degree of difficulty in responding. She started to speak, reconsidered, then started again.

"Much of the information needed to tie the explanation together just isn't there for you yet, because you don't have all your memories available to you. I have faith that all your memories will return, but in the meantime I can provide you with only a superficial explanation. To begin with, there are universal truths, Harry, that are considered by some individuals to be the actual laws of physical existence."

Harry nodded wisely. *"Yes, I understand about universal truths, such as Occam's Razor."*

Ngendo rubbed a smile from her lips. "Yes, that would definitely be one of them. That one and Murphy's Law. The so-called laws I mentioned are a body of knowledge called physics, and there is a subset of physics known as quantum mechanics, and another subset called particle theory. We won't be going into quantum mechanics or particle theory today, but it's an area that had been particularly appealing to you. It's kind of our playground, the two of us.

"As I said, part of what I'll tell you is based on information that is currently locked in your memory. I'm afraid that for now you'll just have to trust me and accept that even though at this time you may not understand how this method of communication works, it does work. There are other methods, but this one will be more consistently useful for you while you're in this bodily configuration."

Harry knew in the abstract that over time he'd had different "bodily configurations", as Ngendo called his physical transformations, but really, all he knew concretely was that he was sorely lacking in thumbs. All the rest of this encounter was more of a flash flood through his mind, and him with only a thin branch to hang onto for survival as he was mentally swept away. He realized in a crystal instant that he did trust Ngendo, and it felt like he had done so for a very long time. He also realized the best thing he could do for now would be to simply relax and allow the flood to flow through him, rather than over him. Ngendo continued, unaware of Harry's consuming insight:

"Since your current body doesn't have the physical construction to vocalize human speech, we necessarily have to use a different method to get the same result. I expect you already know that many beings communicate in some form or other. Some communicate by experiencing a form of intention, or need, to send signals to another being capable of receiving those signals. A male bird may need to attract a mate, so it will use its vocal apparatus to chirp or sing in a certain way to signal its intention to any female birds in the area. Your intention to communicate occurs as a thought in your brain, and that thought is physically expressed in a way particular to you."

It was clear to Ngendo that Harry was struggling to understand what she was saying. "Look, it might be helpful to think of crickets. You know that crickets 'chirp,' right?"

Harry nodded in relief; this was in fact something he did know. Ngendo grasped this small commonality of understanding and built upon it:

"Well, what is really happening is that when a cricket rubs its forewings together, it creates a vibration that is called a sound wave, which travels through the air until it reaches a human ear."

Harry raised a foreleg to interrupt, but Ngendo held up a hand pre-emptively. "I know, I know; you have no idea about sound waves. This is one of those take-it-on-faith parts, then. Trust me that we know sound waves exist, and that after a complex process inside the human body, sound waves are converted into communication that a human can understand. While you obviously aren't a cricket, the physical process is similar. There is intent expressed through a physical process that results in another being receiving a communication. With humans we call that 'hearing.'

"So. Your intention to communicate forms as a thought in your brain. Since you don't currently possess the equivalent of a human vocal apparatus, your brain uses a different physical process to interpret that intention in a manner that causes the hairs on your body to vibrate—to create a sound wave. That sound wave travels through the air to my human ear, and my human brain understands your communication. I 'hear' what you 'said.'"

Harry had learned from Brother Mark the general ins and

outs of religion, such that he recognized a miracle when he saw one. He had so deeply internalized his sorrow at his lack of ability to "properly" communicate that now he felt as if he had been transformed yet again. He would be able to make his true thoughts known; maybe he could achieve friendship with other humans! Ngendo intuited his thoughts and smiled sadly again.

"I think you see this as a great opportunity to make friends and to have a more fulfilling life, and that can be true. But again you must trust me and understand that you must be very cautious and keep in mind how humans see you, at least at first sight. If you randomly speak to them, especially in this age, it will not go well and you will likely put yourself in extreme danger."

Harry's wildly spinning thoughts abruptly stopped, and he realized at once that Ngendo was correct. His remembered experiences with humans in the lifetimes he'd spent in this bodily configuration coalesced into one bitter thought.

"I can 'talk' to humans, but not if I want to remain alive."

"Now, Harry, I don't think it's quite as dire as all that. I'm just saying that you'll need to be even more careful of your safety if you do want to talk to a human, any human. It's easy for even experienced folk like myself to misjudge a situation, to their detriment. Just be cautious."

Harry crossed his two forelegs with a disgruntled *humph. "Well, I cannot say I disagree. Caution is my primary mode of thought, after all. I do not say I understood even a part of what you explained just now, but I have other similarly urgent questions. Why have you come here? What was that mode of travel you used? Why do I see people around us moving so slowly? Why is the ocean so quiet? Where has the wind gone?"*

Ngendo laughed in delight. "Now that's the Harry I know! Let me think a minute."

She carefully straightened her legs in front of her and lifted Harry to her shoulder, then stood and walked to the railing, looking out at the nearly static ocean. There was no breeze and the silence seemed stifling to Harry.

"You know, Harry, when I look at this situation objectively, I can understand how very weird it must seem to you. For me, it's all about understanding the mutability of time and reality and manipulating technology to achieve specific goals."

Her last sentence was so confusing to him that Harry could make no response. Ngendo turned around and leaned back on the railing; he made sure his feet tightly gripped the soft leather of her jerkin. He very sincerely did not wish to fall overboard. She gestured widely with open hands to indicate the area in which they stood.

"Remember, this explanation will be extremely simplistic. Why have I come here? I came because I've been looking for you for a long time and I finally found you. I had lost track of you after your time with The People of the cave." *"What people? I do not remember ever living with people in a cave."*

Ngendo sighed and shook her head, beaded braids softly clicking together. "I know you don't, but let's not worry about that just now. For our current purposes, think of this small area of the deck as being enclosed within a type of vehicle that I can use to travel to different types of locations. Let's call the vehicle a sphere, although that's not what it really is. The technical explanation is much too complex to get through in a short time. Let's just assume that I can travel using such a sphere to nearly any location for which I have the correct settings. *And* return from, that's really important to keep in mind, believe me." She chuckled ruefully at some private memory.

"Anyway, when I travel to *this* type of location, my ability to physically move around the location is restricted to the boundaries of the landing zone. I have to be precise when I'm setting the destination and return information, but I always try to allow a little extra space around the sphere. You're inside the sphere with me now because I purposely extended it to include you when it landed here. I can walk a few steps forward and back, side to side, and the two of us would still be inside the sphere, like so."

To demonstrate, with Harry still on her shoulder Ngendo walked a few paces across the deck to the base of the closest mast, then returned to lean on the railing, arms crossed in front of her and her back to the somnolent ocean waves. Harry felt a little dizzy and tightened his grip on her shoulder again, worried she might forget he was there. She noticed his unease and lightly stroked his back before continuing her explanation. Harry found the stroking comforting.

"For those of us properly licensed to use it, the sphere technology allows us to experience so much, to learn so much. Even though I'm not able to leave the sphere to interact with anything outside the sphere, I *can* interact with whoever happens to be inside the sphere with me, such as your wonderful self."

Ngendo grinned broadly, and Harry tightened his foothold a little more to compensate for possible shoulder movement in case she started laughing again.

"So, we're inside the sphere now. That's the very basic 'how' of me arriving here on this ship. Your perceived-time question is much more complex, of course. You asked why it seems that those people move so very slowly, and why the ocean and wind are so quiet."

She turned to face the ocean and leaned her elbows on the railing. The two of them were quiet for a few moments, absorbing the sight of waves moving so slowly they seemed dense enough to walk across. There was a lone seabird hovering on tilted wings, nearly motionless in the sky. Ngendo took a deep breath.

"I think that's probably the hardest question. The best answer I can offer for now is that while we're inside the sphere, we're essentially in isolation. It's—let's call it a side effect—of the sphere technology that while we're in isolation, all our physical senses operate at a different, um, pace, relative to the environment outside the sphere. Remember I said I can't interact with the environment outside the sphere? Our own physical senses would be disrupted and we'd run the risk of disrupting the pace of time for those outside the sphere."

She shook her head at the thought of such bad behavior by a traveler. Harry struggled to understand but it was hopeless. He was, however, becoming more anxious by the moment. Ngendo continued speaking casually, as if all this information was old news, unaware of Harry's rapidly building dismay.

"Even though we can't sense it ourselves, the beings on the ship outside the sphere still perceive themselves to be peacefully sailing under a clear night sky. They aren't able to perceive the sphere, and our adjusted sense of pace perceives them as moving very slowly."

Harry knew his knowledge and experience were limited, but even so he knew of no type of being that could move throughout the world in this manner. The thought of *demon* persistently refused to fully disperse from his mind. When he spoke, his "voice" rose a few octaves and the tone approached distraught.

"What is this 'pace'? Are you saying that events can occur at different times based on whether you are inside or outside this so-called sphere? How is that possible? Time operates the same for all things, this is not something that can be changed! It seems to me that you are saying you can manipulate time itself. That is not the province of mortal creatures on Earth!"

Harry shivered with unease, not sure whether he could accept Ngendo's explanation. He absolutely did not understand it. His understanding of the universe he inhabited was being broken, and that made him doubt what his own senses were telling him. Ngendo could feel him trembling and stroked him again as she paused to gather her thoughts.

"Harry, please be calm. I know you don't remember me, and I know it's very difficult for you to accept what I say on trust. But believe me that there is no intent to harm anything, or anyone, in any manner. The technology that operates the sphere simply facilitates travel to locations that have a set pace in time, among other types of locations. The technology used by those of us who travel doesn't permit interference with set-pace locations; there are massive protections in place. There's no manipulation of any sort that the technology will allow for those locations."

Ngendo's heart sank when she heard a discreet musical alarm ping for attention. She had been so focused on Harry that she had not kept track of the countdown on her assigned use of the sphere for this visit. She stroked his back again and spoke softly.

"I have to go now, Harry. If you can believe it, the sphere is actually on a timer of sorts. It's unbelievably archaic, I know, but there's a system I have to use and the system has very specific rules. I will visit you again whenever I can. I don't think I'd be able to disrupt a stasis period, but I should be able to reach you otherwise. I can't tell you more than that for now. I want you to remember this, though, if you never remember another thing."

She gazed intently into his eyes, past whatever bodily configurations stood between them, to the being she knew was present in his mind and heart.

"I have found you now and I will not lose you again. I'll be able to find you, but I may not be able to visit you as often as I'd like. I want you to keep your faith in me bright and know that you are my most beloved friend."

She gently lifted Harry from her knee and rose to her feet, then placed him back on the top loop of the rope coil. She walked to the deck railing and Harry saw the portal appear over the water, approaching the ship. He felt something like a wail rise in his chest as he watched it descend to the deck and Ngendo stepped toward it.

"But there is so much more I need to know!"

Ngendo smiled and pointed her index finger at him. "Be assured, I'll be able to find you more easily next time and I'll try to answer more of your questions then. For now, it's not good-bye, but *see you again soon.*"

She turned and stepped through the portal, disappearing, and the portal vanished as silently as it had first appeared.

On the other side of the portal, the airlock hatch quickly closed behind Ngendo with a barely discernable, soft swish. It was but a brief moment or two for the airlock's environmental controls to engage and decontaminate, and another moment to equalize the atmosphere between the airlock and the interior. The inner door opened and she walked down a short corridor, past crew quarters and the small dining/ galley area, then turned into another corridor that ended at the forward control station for the one-person vehicle. There was a discreet chime, the vehicle AI's contrived analog to clearing its nonexistent throat before speaking.

"I assume you found it. Him. Your physical readings are quite high. Are you well?"

Xi's speech tone was a mix of concern for Ngendo and interest in whether the mission was successful. It was fully invested in the mission to find this Harry creature and wanted details of the meeting. Its mission partner's high physical readings were unusual and therefore of some concern, of course, but as there were no critical warnings showing Xi allowed interest to overtake concern. Ngendo grimaced and shook her head.

"Ignore my physical readings, I'm fine. I'm just feeling unhappy and that is being reflected in several physical reactions. It's a human thing. I did find him, and the first meeting was within the mission parameters. The information I gave him may be of some small help to him, I guess. I don't know how he's surviving in that bodily form, though."

Xi observed her partner from multiple monitors as Ngendo removed her outlandish jerkin and savagely threw it to the floor, then kicked it away. She stood for a moment engrossed in thought, then moved alertly to the command station.

"I'm bringing him out with me on the next run. Be told."

Xi didn't have a body configuration that made use of some form of breathing structure, so its gasp of disbelief was a contrived analog of sound.

CHAPTER FOUR

Harry, née Stalker, rapidly shook his head as if awakening from a particularly troubling dream. He raced down the stack of coiled rope, back to his hiding spot under the deck railing. As he scurried for cover, he distractedly worried that he was losing his mind from the dangers and deprivations of the voyage, but a clearer mental voice took over, confirming he had not been dreaming. His reality had been changed temporarily and was now reverting to the one with which he had been familiar. Before he was completely settled in the safety of the deep shadows, his senses had returned to their normal state. He could hear sounds from belowdecks that indicated the colonists were waking. He could feel the soothing rise and fall of the ship as it followed the waves from crest to trough. The faint delineation of ocean from sky was becoming more visible on the horizon, and the night watch began the changeover to the morning watch. He scented the ocean again and could taste the salt in the misty air.

He couldn't understand the lack of ship-sound and ship-movement during the time Ngendo was aboard. Perhaps that was also an effect of *quantum mechanics*. But he could fully recall the alternate reality he had just experienced and could remember the sound of Ngendo's words as if they were being softly spoken to him again. He wanted to take time to study their conversation, to try to understand how it had come to happen. He was resistant to the idea of simply having faith that she'd come back at some unknown time and place. He knew he didn't remember everything about all his past lives, but he couldn't believe he would have forgotten Ngendo. He didn't doubt he'd had the visitation from her, but he did doubt she had been fully truthful with him. Well, maybe she hadn't lacked truthfulness as much as candor. These thoughts were all too frustrating and disruptive for Harry to manage at the moment; he would have to let them simmer in the back of his mind for now.

His twitching nerves had just begun to relax when he saw the ship's cat wandering the deck close by. He had seen the old cat several times during the voyage and thought she looked like she had had some pretty tough lives so far. He caught himself feeling sympathetic toward her. Her ears were missing some bits, her fur was patchy, and she had several scars across her nose and on the top of her head. She didn't normally come up on deck, but she'd caught and eaten all the ship's vermin within the easy kill zones and the rest were rather better at escaping her claws. She'd have to devote more energy to those efforts but that was something for another day. For now, she was merely looking for an out-of-the-way site on deck where she could get out of the wind for a while.

An unusual scent caught her sleepy attention, and she knew something new and different was near. She investigated the railing further, slowly coming closer and closer to Harry. She stopped to give his shadowy hiding place a couple of desultory swipes with a front paw, wondering idly whether this tasty-smelling item might be careless enough to forget she was nearby and show itself. Harry knew the ship's cat couldn't reach him with her paws, but he still felt the air rush past with each of the cat's rapid swipes at him and reflexively cringed farther back in the shadows. This was deeply annoying to him, and really too much to be troubled with after his experience during the night watch. His only excuse for what came next was that he was exhausted, he was hungry and thirsty, and he was severely out of sorts.

Harry had long ago stopped trying to use the same type of communication he had enjoyed with Brother Mark, what he had originally thought of as "mind shouting." During his time with Brother Mark, their thought-sending and receiving became as automatic to Harry, as, well, thinking. When Brother Mark died, Harry had had to train himself out of automatically communicating that way. At the time, there were no other monks who Harry thought were emotionally prepared to experience a disembodied voice in their heads. He would have to wait until someone among the brothers' community became more emotionally progressive, but generations of monks came and went from the monastery while he waited. Eventually he decided to select a monk who he thought could manage such an extraordinary experience and try to reach out to his mind. He tried this a number of times over the years, but without fail, the test subject did not weather it at all well. After several such experiments, Harry had lost count of the number of Hail Marys and other self- imposed penances a test subject felt were required in order to remove the "demonic incursions" they had experienced. Rumors developed that the monastery was haunted, and several exorcisms were held. This would always cause Harry great guilt and remorse, and many years would pass before he'd try again.

Now, however, Harry's self-training in restricted mental communication methodology fell aside, and he angrily mind-shouted at the cat in full mental volume:

"GO AWAY!"

As the shouted thought left his mind, Harry abruptly remembered first meeting the monastery's cat, Saint James, under similar circumstances. During that meeting, Saint James had held him down with a paw, which so annoyed Harry that he mind-shouted at the cat very loudly, which resulted in Saint James taking a short, unexpected flight. Appearing to move in slow motion, Saint James had lifted into the air, all four legs and tail stiff, every hair on his body standing straight out, looking like a type of forest shrub. Harry could smell a blended aroma of singed fur and the sharp ozone odor of a lightning strike. When Harry mind-shouted at Saint James, he had unintentionally added a powerful jolt of his body's stored energy, which had fueled the cat's flight across Brother Mark's chamber.

The current scene played out very differently. The ship's cat was apparently somewhat startled by the mind shout, yes, but her career as ship's cat had made her tough and not so susceptible to her prey's drama. As well, she hadn't been touching Harry so there was no energy transmitted between bodies along with Harry's vehemently shouted thought. Instead of hissing and running away, she yawned theatrically and sat back on her haunches, her head tilted alertly to the side. This was an interesting development; truth be told, a ship's cat experienced long stretches of absolute boredom. Sleeping nearly all the time alleviated quite a bit of that boredom, but if she slept any more the sailors were likely to throw her overboard for being dead. She wasn't necessarily against swimming but preferred it to be at her own election.

Harry felt limp and worn out. He could see that his mind-shout hadn't affected the cat, but at least it had made it quit swiping at him. Unfortunately, from its posture he felt it still looked interested in him. He knew the ship's cat was a skilled ambush hunter, and that his future foraging efforts were potentially going to be even more complicated. He wouldn't be able to stay hidden until the ship reached landfall; he would need food and water long before then. He thought grimly that his only option was to attempt a détente, but first he scrunched himself even farther back into his hiding place, just in case this cat had a longer reach. He turned his mental volume way down and reached out again.

"Would it perhaps be possible for the two of us to cease hostilities, at least temporarily, and exchange names?" The ship's cat yawned again, idly licked a front paw,

and casually washed its face. Harry saw this for the irritating performance it was and did not relax his attention. He had to be ready to run in case there was an opportunity to escape. The ship's cat put its paw down and tilted its head to the other side, then spoke in a musing tone.

*I suppose anything is possible, but whether or not a thing is probable is the better question. Is it *possible* I could refrain from pursuing you? Of course, as I said, anything is possible, but is it *probable*? I *am* just a cat with instincts, you know.*

Harry snorted rudely at that. *"There is no such thing as 'just a cat,' with or without instincts. I am well aware that you are at the top of the non-human food chain on board this ship, whereas I unfortunately occupy a much lower link in that chain. If we were on dry land, I would wager you would still be substantially near the top, but I would have additional options for escape. I have no intention of participating in your cat-career, on or off this ship. Even so, shall we at least introduce ourselves? My name is St—er, Harry."*

The cat thought about this. The wind had picked up and was ruffling her fur, not something she greatly enjoyed. This interaction was turning out to require more energy than she felt like donating to it; a comfy bed of ragged, used sailcloth was on her mind. *Very well. I am simply called Catt.*

Harry flipped up a sarcastic foreleg. *"Of course, what else would you be called? Fine. I would say I am pleased to meet you, but I fear that will have to wait until I feel I am not so close to being your midmorning snack."*

Catt took no offense at Harry's tone and opened her mouth in an even more cavernous yawn that looked to Harry like she had swallowed her head backwards. He was interested to see that Catt was missing a few teeth and one of her fangs was broken off. Apparently she'd been a ship's cat for a very long time indeed. She closed her mouth after yawning and blinked twice.

I would stay and talk further, but I am weary and rough weather is coming in, youngster. I need to get to a place where the waves will not reach me. She turned to go, limping a little on a back paw. "As new things are rare, in my experience, I have found it is not a best practice to simply eat them as a first reaction. I find you interesting and I am not opposed to getting to know each other. We shall continue this conversation another time, St-er-Harry.*

Harry was glad to see her leaving, until what she said made it past his nerves to his understanding. *"Wait. What do you mean, so the waves will not reach you? The waves stay mostly on the outside of the ship, even during storms."* He thumped the rail with a back leg. *"This is a good, solid ship."*

Catt paused and looked back over her shoulder, a pitying expression on her face. *Child, is this is your first ocean voyage?*

"I think so. I am unsure. I unexpectedly found myself on this ship a short time before it was launched on this voyage. I have since deduced that I am an unwitting stowaway, as I had hidden in the

body of tree that was apparently shipped here and then turned into the rearward mast. I can only pray that this is the last time I find myself on an ocean voyage, witting or otherwise."

Catt laughed so hard she had to sit back down, facing Harry. *Oh my. The storms we have sailed through so far on this voyage were infants compared to the one that is chasing us now. Can you not smell it? I can tell that this storm will be bad, and it is coming very fast. It is quite possible this may not only be your last ocean voyage, it may turn out to be your last anything. Do you not see the monstrous black clouds racing toward us?*

Harry normally didn't pay much attention to the daytime sky; his interest was in the night sky information provided by the moon and stars. He saw now that the morning sky had turned an unhealthy-looking greenish purple color and the clouds appeared to be boiling, becoming thicker by the minute. He became aware then of the rapidly increasing wind, and the shouts of the sailors as they hustled about securing the deck for rough weather. The mainsails were stowed, but there was no time to rig the storm sails. The crew's quick and precise actions weren't driven by panic, but Harry could see the deep concern on their faces. Everyone but the working sailors was sent below. Catt still sat in front of him, gazing at him inquiringly.

"Can the waves truly rise over the ship? Are we in danger of the coming storm sinking the ship? What should we do?"

The ship was heading into waves of increasing size, but it seemed to Harry that the crew was still in control of the ship. Catt sighed, then stood and shifted her stance to compensate as the pitch of the deck rose sharply, then fell back to a lower starting point. Harry could feel the tension and anxiety of the sailors rising in tandem with the increasing height of the waves.

The truth is, child, any ship is in danger of sinking any time it rides the waves. Anything can happen. Death can result in situations from the smallest inattention to a task, to the effects of the most dreadful storm. A sailor's life can be lost in a heartbeat, and this is something they—we—all understand. This is a fact of sailing life.

Catt turned her face into the rapidly strengthening wind and had her whiskers blown back. She lifted her nose into the wind, her mangled ears standing even more erect, tail lashing behind her.

Indeed, a storm comes, a very bad one. Be aware, child, that it is unusual we have come this far mostly unharmed. Normally at least some damage or other problem would have happened several times by now. I heard the captain say we are less than two days out from our intended port, so we shall see if this storm changes our destinies.

This was not good news to Harry. He thought the voyage thus far had been exceedingly difficult and had a hard time imagining a worse situation. He strongly felt it was unlikely, regardless of the number of his previous lives, that he had ever been a sailor. He noted that for his future lives, if he were to have any, he intended to remain firmly on land, given a choice. To his surprise, Catt quickly jumped into the center of the stack of coiled rope, landing lightly and without warning. She stood on her hind legs looking out at Harry in his hiding place, her front paws on the top of the coiled loops.

Come here, child, if you would survive the storm! We will be as safe in here as anywhere now. We do not want to be trapped belowdecks.

Harry left his usual caution behind and scrambled down from the railing and over to the rope stack. Mentally berating himself for being a fool, he quickly climbed the outside of the stack to where Catt waited. She dropped down into the interior of the coiled loops and gestured for Harry to join her. He left himself drop down beside her, holding his breath. When he landed, she swept a foreleg around him and gathered him in close to her body, curling up tightly. He was inclined to resist, but her fur smelled of clean ocean air and she was very warm. Catt began purring and gently licked his head a couple of swipes, which tickled his ears. Inexplicably, Harry felt safe with Catt sheltering him.

Within minutes, a horrendous darkness swept over the ship, suffusing any hint of daylight. They heard cries of *"hurricane"* and now it seemed there was panic, as the crew rushed to tie themselves to the masts, to the railings, to anything they hoped would keep them from being washed overboard. The ship's prow was turned to face the storm and the wind howled across the ship, causing the rigging to shriek like a thing in pain. The captain screamed at the helmsman to keep the ship at an angle to the waves, hoping to save it from being swamped by the massive weight of the water repeatedly crashing over it. The height of the waves doubled, then doubled again. The heavy air was abruptly electrified and lightning struck the masthead, sending flaming slabs of wood crashing to the deck. Harry and Catt felt the impact beneath them, and Harry realized that to be carried away from the ship was to die. If they were swept overboard Catt would most certainly die, and perhaps even he would die. He was startled to realize that dying did not hold the attraction for him just then that it sometimes did.

Harry huddled deeper into Catt's fur and listened to the sharp creaking of the ship's timbers as each monstrous wave smashed over the prow. They were nearly deafened by the sound of the screaming wind and the thunder of opaque sheets of rain thrashing across the ship. The open top of the rope coil didn't stop the heavy rain from reaching them, and it struck Catt with such force that she cried out. The rain didn't touch Harry, but he could feel Catt's body trembling. He tried to reach past his own terror to Catt's mind to provide her with some measure of comfort, but the physical and emotional stresses on both of them made that impossible.

The helmsman strove mightily at the wheel at the stern of the ship, trying to hold the rudder in place to keep the ship's prow headed aslant the waves. The wind was a living, shrieking demon that forced him to his knees, as if he were praying to the god of storms to save the ship, to save him. The old pagan gods were never far away when the sailors' usual God left them to the mercies of another god's storms. The wheel spun madly, and the helmsman's arm was caught between the spokes and broken as he screamed for help. He had lashed himself to the wheel mast and could not free himself. The captain, lashed to a railing nearby but out of reach of the wheel, frantically tried and failed to cut the rope that would ultimately save his own life. There was nothing more to be done but for the crew to hold fast where possible and ride out the storm.

The ship was thrust up the heaving vertical fronts of the nightmarish waves, each wave cresting higher than the last. It was driven down into the trough between the waves, angling deeper into the trough each time until it seemed the ship would flip end over end. The waves crashed over the ship mere seconds apart, giving neither ship nor crew time to regroup before being inundated again. With the wheel and rudder stricken, the ship's heading drifted so that instead of the prow leading the ship into the waves, the ship slipped sideways and brought its starboard side almost parallel with the next series of waves. A wall of water taller than a cathedral slammed down over the ship, swamping it, and heaving it over on its port side, so that it seemed it would come to lie flat in the water.

The rope stack began to slowly slide across the deck, until it reached the tensile limits of the smaller ropes tying it to the deck cleats, where it was stopped and held. As the ship's roll continued, the stack's side bindings held it together as it left the deck and dangled in the air for a moment. But the bindings that tied it to the deck cleats couldn't hold the stack's weight. Catt and Harry, huddled inside it, clearly heard a *snap* even above the roaring wind as the bindings gave way.

You must be brave, child—we are going down. We will try to save ourselves. You must use all those legs to swim. If you see a floating piece of this poor ship you must climb onto it and hold onto it for your life.

The rope stack fell from the ship, along with many other shipboard items that had broken loose and were about to become flotsam and jetsam in the water. Within the stack, Catt huddled against the side and tried to hold onto the rough rope with all of her claws, while Harry tried to hold onto Catt with all of his legs. When the stack hit the ocean surface, the impact caused the ropes holding it together to burst apart, releasing Catt and Harry from its interior to face continuing terrors. The rope uncoiled as it sank, like a monstrous snake leaving its nest. Ship debris slammed into the water.

Harry couldn't see daylight and didn't know if he was upside down or right-side up. He had no idea what it meant to swim; he had never seen anyone or anything swim. He determined immediately that he couldn't breathe, and that it was preferable to be above the water rather than below it. He reflexively struck out with the claw at the end of a foreleg and brushed against the rope. He grabbed it as it drifted past him, but instead of sinking with the rope he climbed it in what he considered an upwards direction. He climbed up as fast as he could, but it wasn't enough. His lungs were simply too small to hold enough air for him to make it to the surface. His body convulsed, and the rope slipped away from him. He breathed deeply of the water, convulsed again, then was limp.

Suddenly something grabbed Harry by his rear legs and pulled him up sharply. His mind was rapidly darkening, but he was still able to feel puzzled. He thought something was probably going to eat him but he hadn't been torn asunder or swallowed just yet. With his last sight fading, he glimpsed sparkling light above his head. Then he knew nothing more.

Harry's foreleg twitched, and he moaned piteously. He became aware that he was lying on a wide piece of wood floating on the ocean surface, feeling extremely thirsty and very broken. The board was large enough that while water lapped over the ragged, broken edges, it didn't reach the center where he lay sprawled under the mercilessly broiling sun. Harry forced his legs to move and managed to shakily stand. His sight was blurred, his body crusted with salt. He gingerly rubbed his eyes with his forelegs, dislodging salt crystals, and was able to see a little better. His senses were dull, but he thought the storm had passed. The board bobbed on ocean swells that bore no resemblance to the demonic waves that had caused the ship to roll. There was no sign of the ship.

Catt lay stiffly on her side nearby, looking even more battered than Harry felt. He feared she was dead, but he saw her sides move as she took in shallow breaths. He crawled weakly across the board to her and sat near her head, not knowing what he could do to help her or to at least make her more comfortable. He didn't usually despise his own body, but there were times when he wished with all his heart his body was shaped in a manner that could move as humans moved. He realized that what he had felt grab him and pull him to the surface must have been Catt. She had saved his life. Harry tentatively patted her head and her eyelid twitched. He patted her cheek a little harder and she opened an eye. Then she opened her other eye as well and lifted her head, coughing weakly. She pushed up with her front legs and managed to sit up, looking groggily around.

Well, child, I see that we are not at the bottom of the sea. What I do not see is the ship.

Harry looked around as well, just in case he had missed a sail or two.

"*I just became conscious and saw you, but I did not see the ship.*" He paused, strangely inclined to wring the claws at the ends of his forelegs, as he had seen humans wring their hands in distress. "*What are we to do?*"

Catt shook her ears and lay back down with her front legs stretched in front of her. She half-heartedly licked the crusted fur on a paw, grimacing at the intense taste of salt.

If I were to be cruel, I would say we are to die. However, we may yet survive. Do you see the faint haze on the horizon?

Harry rubbed his eyes again and squinted in the direction Catt had indicated. There was an indistinct line of blue that was differentiated from both the ocean surface and the azure of the sky.

"*I can barely make it out, but I see something. What is it?*"

That, child, is where our lives may be saved if we can but get to it. It is land. I believe the storm blew the ship landward, but to which land I do not know. If we are very lucky, this board floats with the current that runs to the ship's intended port. I do not think we were that far from it when the storm came. Such storms often travel along coastlines. Harry wasn't inclined to think luck would help them.

"How long have we been stranded on this wood? Is there no way to ensure we stay with the current, or to travel more quickly? Could we not paddle from the sides of this raft?"

Catt coughed again, and it was a few moments until she had breath to continue speaking.

*I think this is the end of the same day the storm took us. I am too weak to try paddling anything. Even if I could, and I mean you no offense, you would not be able to help move this board. However, *if* that haze is land, and *if* we float on the correct current, and *if* there is not another storm, I expect this board will meet that shore by the next sunset. We shall try to stay alive until then.*

This brief conversation consumed her small reserve of strength, and she stretched out on her side again, exhausted.

Wake me when it looks like we will crash into the rocks. We could hope for a smooth sandy beach for washing ashore, but I suspect that is not what Fate wishes to observe.

Catt's words did nothing to alleviate Harry's upset at being shipwrecked. He'd heard the sailors' wild tales of castaways who were never seen again, but yet the storytellers improbably knew the fate of said castaways. Aggressive, unreasonable natives figured large in some tales, while other stories were loaded with buried treasure and all the rum a sailor could drink. There was a night when Harry had surreptitiously sipped a spilled drop or two of a sailor's daily rum allotment and decided that he could do pretty well without it. He considered now that perhaps if there were a drop or two of rum available, he wouldn't turn it down. Rum was mostly water without salt.

Catt's extreme lethargy worried him. Her breathing sounded rough and wet, like her lungs contained more seawater than air. She was much closer to the edge of the board than he liked, but there was no way he could move her. He bitterly remembered sitting by the bed of the last monk to die of the pestilence, helpless to do anything besides watch and pray. Prayer was always good, but—what if—A thought had occurred to him. Catt obviously wasn't ill with the pestilence; she had nearly drowned and was weakly struggling to breathe. He went over to her and gently crept onto her side. Her whiskers twitched but that was all the indication she gave of being aware of Harry sitting on her. He steadied himself and made sure each of his feet touched the skin beneath her damp fur. He felt her chest rattle as her ribcage rose to eke out each shallow breath.

Brother Mark had taught him a process to help ready his mind for prayer, and Harry had become an adept practitioner. He closed his eyes and listened to the sounds around him, felt the ocean breeze, tasted the salt air. The heat of the sun beat upon him. He isolated each sensation, then dismissed it from his consciousness, until finally there was nothing in his mind but himself. Within that dark quiet he reached out and sought Catt's life energy, finding only a very dim point of far-distant light. As he focused his attention on it, the tiny pinpoint flickered. He knew there was very little time left before it faded completely, and he would be alone. He searched for a way to sustain it, but he was weak himself and couldn't extend his energy far enough to reach it. He could feel despair edging back into his consciousness and thrust it away.

Harry had used concentrated energy only once that he recalled, and the use had been reactive and inadvertent. He couldn't remember purposely calling upon such energy, but he knew that didn't mean he never had. He calmed himself, and deeply focusing his intention, he formed the thoughts *Find!*

and *Remember!* then sent them hunting. In but an instant, he saw in his mind a memory of knowledge and experience:

All things in the universe vibrate individually, and the universe vibrates in turn as a collective whole. Vibrations manifest as energy that can be discerned in some manner. He remembered being able to see the energy emanating not only from living things, but also inanimate things like rocks and soil, albeit the energy from non-living matter is barely notable. Now that he knew what there was to find, he cast about with his mind's eye and found energy manifesting around him. It swirled around him in the air, in the water, in the life of the sea, and it was his to use.

Harry made of himself a tiny conduit, and very carefully fed a molecule-wide filament of energy toward the pinpoint of light in the distance, which was all that remained of Catt's life-force. The filament touched the pinpoint and the intensity of the small light grew, as did its size. Bright energy slowly began to flow from that instantiation to form an internal framework inside the cat, bringing oxygen-laden blood cells to bear on fading organ strength. Harry remained still for some time, steadying the flow when necessary, watching her body make such repairs as it could, until finally Catt gave a deep sigh and stretched her legs. She appeared to be sleeping naturally, her breathing easy now, her ribcage rising and falling smoothly. Harry gradually slowed the energy flow and gently withdrew into his own consciousness. It surprised him to realize that he felt better himself.

He didn't feel as thirsty and his own energy level seemed higher than it had been even aboard the ship. The intensity of the sun blazing on his collector "eyes" had given him a rapid reset, but without actual food and water that reset wouldn't last long. He moved away from Catt a little and settled into a crouch. He drowsily watched the waves move; the repetitive motion was hypnotic and strangely soothing. So different from storm waves! He remembered Catt had mentioned a current that might take them landward. Harry hadn't learned much about ocean currents, having only the information he had overheard the sailors discussing. He observed the sun descending to the horizon and knew that direction was westward. The large piece of wood they occupied was moving toward the setting sun, and the purple haze that indicated land was becoming more distinct. The night air chilled them both as they slept through the night.

Harry woke with a scrambling jerk and saw Catt sitting upright near the forward edge of the board. The sky was quickly lightening with the rising sun, which was at their backs. The board spun gently, gathering foam at the edges, and Harry realized the underside was scraping across a surface covered with only an inch or two of water. Catt had heard him move and turned her head to speak to him over her shoulder.

It is timely you are awake, child. It seems that Fate prefers a smooth sandy beach for those of us washing ashore. Let us see if this new land includes fresh water and a few vermin.

Catt gently picked Harry up with her mouth and gracefully leaped off the board onto the sand. She trotted a few meters farther up the beach and set him down in a small patch of shade. He was intensely grateful for the immediately cooler air. Catt gave him a quick lick on the top of his head and sat beside him, looking around with interest.

*Let us welcome each other to what may well be *La Florida*, child.*

PART SEVEN

E lena moves back slightly from the side of Harry's aquarium and considers Bakari sitting on the floor beside her. Now that Harry's conscious, the tension level of the humans in the room has fallen accordingly. We all look exhausted, but I would call Bakari's expression soul sick; it's well beyond guilty and out the other side. I feel a little guilty myself. Now that my fear for Harry has been relieved for the most part, I can see just how young she is. I look back to Harry and notice that he's doing what looks like mantis yoga— stretching all his legs and checking wing deployment effi- ciency. Luckily for me, Elena takes point on dealing with Bakari. She rubs the girl's shoulder gently and smiles at her, then clearly makes a command decision.

"Instead of us immediately running for home and leaving you here alone, why don't we all take a little break to decom- press. I could use a cup of coffee and maybe a cookie or two."

Bakari looks at her gratefully and wipes her teary eyes again. "I could totally put together a nice snack for us. Could we go to the kitchen? It's friendlier than sitting in the dining room. I can make coffee and see what there is to eat."

I see Harry stop his flexing and consider the offer. I assume he'll want to strike visiting off the agenda and get out of Dodge sooner than later, but as usual he surprises me.

"If Tristan and Elena are okay with that, I believe I would like some refreshments after all." He tilts his head to the side and shrugs. "I'm feeling stronger by the minute, and it is probably a good idea to tell them at least a brief recap of the last couple of days."

Bakari looks even more upset at that, and Elena pats her again. Harry flits his wings and leaves the aquarium, landing on my shoulder. I twist my head sideways and grin at him while he's getting his feet settled. I'll be Captain Obvious here and say that this result is so much better than the scenarios Elena and I had feared. It looks like maybe no one will be going to jail. I unfold my benumbed legs and ungracefully stand up, then offer a hand to Elena and assist her to her feet. Bakari, being youthfully indestructible, jumps up on her own. She's really motivated to redeem herself, and I can't blame her. We're truly blessed her plans for Harry didn't pan out.

I pick up the aquarium and place it out of the way on the top of the trunk, then slide the trunk back to its place against the foyer wall. Bakari gestures for us to follow her and leads us through a short hallway that goes through to the back of the house and ends at the kitchen. This house may be old- fashioned, but the large kitchen is exceedingly modern and thoroughly equipped. They could easily feed a platoon from here. Bakari sees me salivating over the equipment and grins. "Pretty cool, right? My parents like to entertain so we have company for dinner and on the weekends a lot. I'm just starting to shadow our cook to see how she makes all the food. She's really good with fancy recipes and everyday food, too."

Bakari clearly knows her way around the kitchen and soon there is hot coffee sitting in front of us, and baked goods warming in the microwave. Harry doesn't have his usual china cup, but Bakari finds a sewing thimble that works, although it looks a bit awkward for him. We take a quiet minute to sample our coffee and work on tension release. Bakari clears her throat and focuses on her coffee cup, holding it in both hands. Elena looks at me and lifts an eyebrow, which I take to mean I should stay quiet for now. Bakari hunches her shoulders and seems to shrink in on herself as she starts to speak.

"Well." She clears her throat again. "I explained this to Harry in more detail, but I'll give you the short version because I know you all want to go home pretty soon. I have a neurological condition that causes me to hallucinate, and sometimes it's like I'm living in an alternate reality, like I'm watching other people's lives. Except some of the lives seem to be from a really long time ago, and I can almost feel everything the people feel. Even though I thought things were getting better, the hallucinations started being even more intense. At first it was like I was watching a movie, but gradually that changed. Now I can hear things. Sometimes I can almost taste food and smell flowers. I've seen some pretty violent things happen to people in the hallucinations, and I worry that I'll also start feeling pain. Even worse, the hallucinations have gotten much longer and more intense. Sometimes I can't break out of them."

She twists her hands in distress. "I really think I could die from them."

I can feel my eyebrows trying to climb up my forehead and glance at Harry, but he's studiously ignoring me. I force my attention back to Bakari.

"Anyway, the only thing that seemed to help get the hallucinations under control was if I could completely focus on something else. Unfortunately, this time I focused on Harry."

Elena nods. "You held off the hallucinations by obsessively focusing on something that took all your mental energy. It kept you in "the now," if you will. For a time, there was no mental energy left for the hallucinations to manifest in your mind."

Bakari looks at her in surprised gratitude. "Yes, exactly! Except this time, I ended up hurting someone because I didn't understand what they are." She looks down again, visibly ashamed. "I'm so sorry, but I don't know if I can ever make it up to Harry."

After listening to Bakari candidly explain her condition, the rest of my rapidly diminishing ire with her finally and fully dissipates. If I've learned anything from Harry, it's the beneficial nature of compassion and forgiveness. I have questions and dare Elena's ire by speaking.

"I get that Harry got shocked by the keypad and accidentally called out the local militia, but what happened to you? How did you end up in the hospital?"

The girl tiredly rubs her eyes, and I think it's just about time to call it a day. "It's so weird. I don't remember anything, other than one minute I'm talking to Harry, and the next I'm waking up as I'm being put in an ambulance."

Harry sets his thimble down. "I can give some insight there. It has to do with me manipulating energy flows, which I'll explain. Briefly."

Ah. I have a feeling I know where this is going. Harry still isn't looking at me, but he has our complete attention.

He's focused intently on Bakari; he seems different somehow, maybe less innocent—more adult. Maybe this adventure has affected him more than we realized. Bakari seems mesmerized by his gaze as Harry starts speaking to her in an oddly intent manner:

"Bakari, to begin this explanation, first and seemingly so obvious, I am not a human being. Nor am I currently an insect, of any sort. I currently only appear to be such an animal. Do you understand?"

Bakari smiles a little, as we all do, and nods hesitantly, but it's clear she's confused by this beginning. Harry folds his arms in front of him and contemplatively looks down for a moment, then back up at the girl.

"I have had, let's call them life experiences, that are far too extensive and obscure to delve into now. I don't have all my memories, but to my current recollection I am not an alien life-form. I developed, over time, here on Earth. To my knowledge there is no other being like myself currently alive on Earth, but of course I don't know all there is to know. There could be others like me, but I doubt they exist."

She nods again and starts to speak, but Harry waves a mitten to quiet her. He smiles a little mantis smile at her and continues.

"I'll allow questions at the end. For now, I simply want to provide information. Okay? So, we can assume we know what I'm *not*, but we don't know what I *am*. Some of the information I'm going provide you'll have to take on faith, unfortunately, since it's not observable in this reality."

All our eyebrows go up at that. I think I understand what Harry said, but I hadn't thought that experiencing some of his memories with him was observing an alternate reality. I probably have as many questions as Bakari at this point.

Elena has never had the directly shared memory experience with Harry, but she and I have had the alternate reality discussion any number of times as a diverting thought exercise. Usually after a few drinks. I get my attention back to Harry.

"I am an unusual being, and I have unusual capabilities. Over time, I have developed the ability to perceive and to direct ambient energy flows for specific purposes—"

Bakari can't make herself be quiet and excitedly interrupts. "Oh my God, are you a *superhero*?"

Harry appears utterly flabbergasted. "What? Of course I'm not a superhero—*that's* what you're getting out of this, that I'm a superhero?"

"Well, yeah. You know, energy beams and everything. All superheroes have special powers. I'm a famous geek on social media, I should have guessed that right away about you."

Harry waves his arms in frustrated negation and retakes the conversation. "No, no, no. Remember I said questions at the end? You need to hear the whole explanation first."

She settles back into her chair and we all take a beat to gather our thoughts. Harry paces back and forth a few steps across the tabletop, then stops in front of Bakari again. A glint catches my eye and I see that the solar collectors on his back are more iridescent than usual.

"Again, and hopefully with no further interruptions, I can perceive and direct energy flows." He gives Bakari a very dry look. "And I only use my powers for good."

She laughs out loud and triumphantly points a finger at him in recognition of his use of the trope's most famous line. Harry shakes his head but he does smile.

"Anyway, my use of energy is the baseline information for explaining your experience, Bakari. You are correct that we were in the midst of our conversation when things changed. You suddenly became rigid and toppled to the floor beside the chair in which you had been sitting. You were non-responsive to my questions but were very clearly in distress. You were having a seizure, and I feared for your well-being. I felt I had to do something to help you."

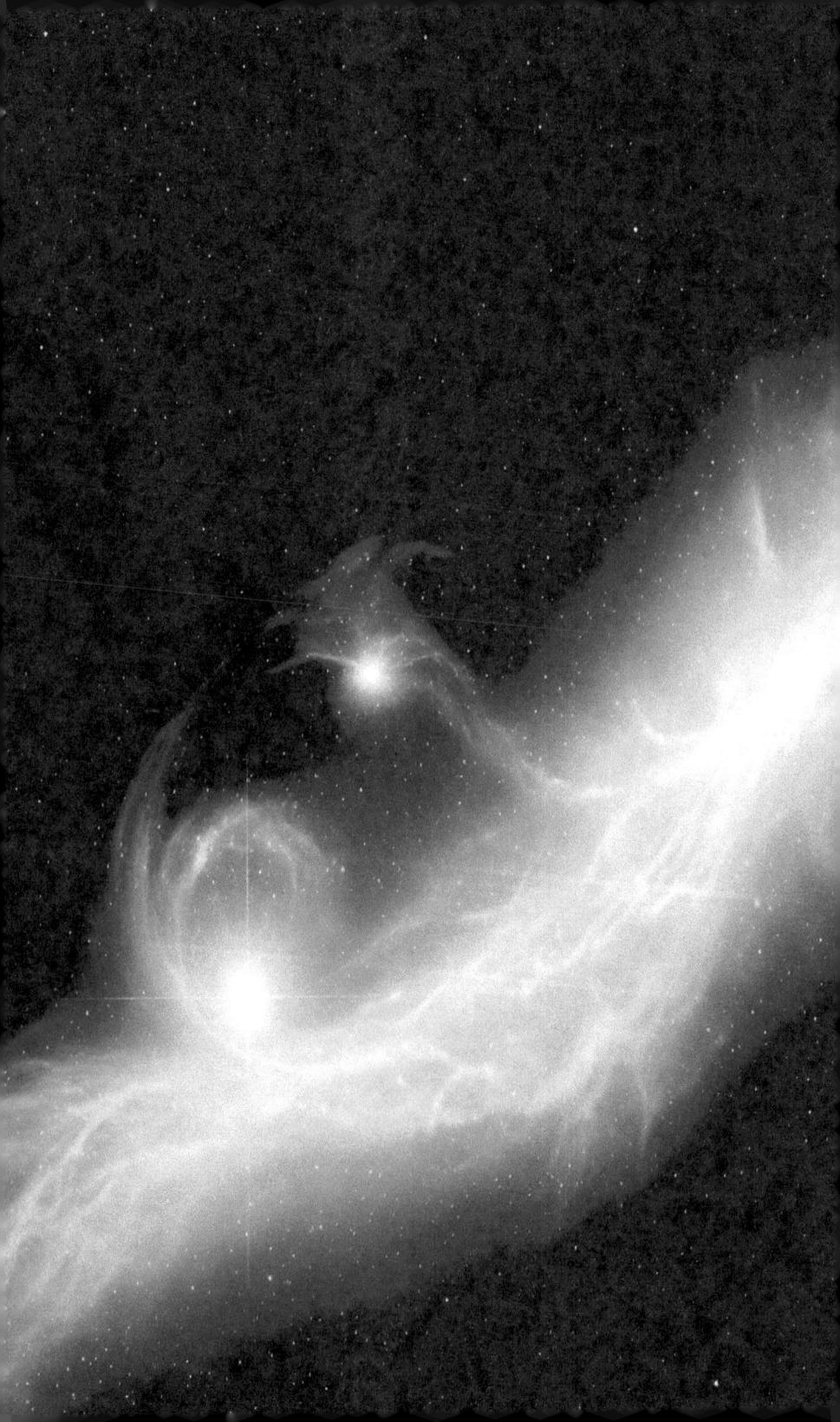

Bakari's dark eyes are impossibly wide, and her attention is utterly focused on Harry, as if they are the only two beings in the room. Elena and I scarcely dare to breathe. Harry glances sideways at me without moving his head and blinks once, as if sending a message. I suddenly realize Bakari is not going to get the whole story, at least not today. Perhaps never.

"I can see and adjust the energy fields of a living body, Bakari. I regret that it's too complicated to try to explain further just now. I could see that, in one very small, particular spot at the very back of your brain, the energy didn't appear to be flowing correctly. That constriction seemed to be causing the seizure you were having.

"I simply smoothed out the knot, so to speak, which allowed the energy in that area to flow correctly. The seizure immediately stopped, and you fell into a normal sleep pattern. Because of the way the energy repair stopped the seizure I doubt you'll have further hallucinations, but I would recommend you still be cautious with your health. Take things slowly for a while."

The girl's eyes close and she sways in her chair. Elena stands and reaches out to steady her, and I rise to go stand beside her as well. Bakari is shaking and I see tears on her cheeks. After a moment or two, Bakari sits up and wipes her face with a napkin Elena hands her from the table. Elena and I return to our seats; Bakari needs another few minutes to recover. Harry stands calmly in his same place before her. Bakari looks at Harry with luminous eyes.

"How can I thank you? You've given me the chance for a life I've never had and never thought I could have. After what I did to you—"

Harry waves that off with a shrug. "I have to say, I am grateful things turned out as they have. I wasn't prepared to exit this particular experience just yet. Life is dangerous, and it happens as it happens. What remains is how we manage the situations in which we find ourselves, and what we learn from our experiences. I now have a deeper understanding that humans can be driven to actions in ways I did not previously understand. Some, certainly not all, of those actions can be life-threatening to others but may not have been carried out with malicious intent to harm. Regardless of intent, there are always consequences."

That gets our full attention; Bakari looks understandably worried.

"Yes, I understand. I will try my best to do whatever you want me to do."

He shrugs again, but his look at her is uncompromising. I feel a strange worry; I don't recognize this version of Harry. Something has changed in him.

"You must give me your promise, on your honor, that you will never discuss, mention, write of, display, or otherwise convey any information about me, in any way or by any method. Even, and especially, with your family. Do you think you can do that?"

She nods emphatically. "That is so not a problem. I sort of assumed that would be a requirement. I promise, pledge, vow, whatever you need. Do you want me to take an oath on a Bible, like they do in court? I mean human court? I could probably find a Bible around here somewhere. Wow, this is so cool, this is just like one of the role-playing games I play with my friends!"

And just like that, the teenager is back. Harry finally lightens up a little and laughs. I turn my own chortle into a cough behind my hand.

"No, I don't need to have you take an oath on a Bible. Your solemn vow is enough for me. I think at this point we can trust each other."

Bakari gives that her due consideration, but then it seems there's a complication. "The only thing is, how do I explain to my parents what happened with me ending up in the hospital? When I called them from the ER they got the very short version of the story, but trust me, they're going to want details."

Elena pats Bakari's hand. "Do we assume correctly that your family doesn't know you, um, obtained Harry for your research?"

"No, they don't know anything about that. And they never come up to my lab area since it's kind of my own private area in the house. Plus I think it creeps them out, but they never say so."

Another pat. "As well it should, sweetheart. Perhaps this is research you won't need to continue, and you'll just observe animals in their living environments?"

Bakari nods fervently. "Absolutely, never again!" "Now, understand that we really don't want to put you in the position of lying to your family and friends. People generally agree that a person can tell lies by omitting information, but sometimes we might need to apply reason and discretion to limit the information we share. There are times when information might be held back to keep someone safe. I believe that a person should be as honest as they can reasonably be, but I also believe that not all information is good for everyone to know."

I can't help myself. "Whew, that is for sure. I guess that goes for posting people's photos on social media, yes?"

Elena blushes a little. "Yes, of course, Tristan. I know I carry as much responsibility for this situation as anyone. I'll be deleting everything about Harry from my account as soon as we get home. For now, though, I think we need Bakari to truthfully tell her parents as much as she can, but without mentioning anything about Harry. It's a tricky situation, I know.

"But let's think this through. It's true that Bakari was working in her lab, doing research, looking over her notes and so forth, and there's no need to mention Harry as being part of any of that. It's also true that she had a distressing physical event occur. It may have been a hallucination, but we don't actually know the cause of the distress. Whatever it was, the event caused her to feel unwell, again also true."

Elena looks around the table, then folds her hands in her lap. "This is the part I'm less than comfortable with, though. We can't truthfully explain what really set off the house alarms without mentioning Harry. We do need to credibly explain how the aid crews were called, and why Bakari was subsequently taken to the hospital."

Bakari puts her elbow on the table and props her chin in her hand; she looks fascinated.

"This is so cool, it's like a spy novel or something.

Maybe we say someone broke in looking for secret information and set everything off? But they had the wrong house?"

I get the sense from Elena rubbing her forehead that even her patience may have limits. Harry looks noncommittal—he's already said his piece. I'm fascinated myself and wonder who might blow up first. Elena takes a sip of her coffee, which has to be cold by now, before she continues to speak.

"No, Bakari, part of what we need to do is stay with the actual facts as much as possible and not just make up a story. I was thinking that we simply say that because you were feeling unwell and were alone, you took out your phone to call 911 but instead you accidentally set off the keypad alarms before passing out. The alarms called out police, fire, and rescue teams. The EMTs found you lying semi-conscious upstairs and took you to the hospital emergency room."

I raise a hand to add my observation. "I don't think you need to mention Elena or me, either. I think we'd be kind of hard to explain without connecting us to Harry somehow."

Bakari rolls her eyes at me. "No doubt. I assumed the *fatwa* on mentioning Harry extended to you guys. So, okay, I signed myself out of the hospital, but how was I supposed to have gotten home?"

I shrug. "You called a taxi?"

She nods. "Yes, that would work in theory, but there are records of taxi fares. You know this story will fall apart real quick if anyone digs into it?"

I'm dumbfounded yet again, which is turning out to be a common feeling for me the past couple of days. "Okay, just to level set, this isn't a spy novel or role-playing game. There's no reason anyone should feel the need to investigate, right? So taking a taxi is okay, right?"

Elena pats my hand this time, but Bakari just snickers at me.

"I'm just messing with you, relax. Fine, I'll say I grabbed a taxi." She sighs and shrugs. "This is a little more complicated anyway because I was supposed to have gone to my uncle's house after my aunt had to leave. I wasn't supposed to have been alone, so I'll definitely get some kind of parental consequence for that at least. The fact that I ended up going to the hospital will only add to the overall doom coming my way." She fidgets a bit, looking down at her coffee cup.

"Um. I don't suppose there's any way I could stay in touch with you all? I mean maybe we could meet for coffee or something once in a while? If I'm ever allowed out of the house again. I know Harry couldn't have a coffee date with me, but you could let me know how he's doing. Maybe one of you could text me sometimes or something?"

She sounds so wistful that Elena stands and pulls Bakari up into a big hug.

"Don't worry, we'll figure something out. People with common interests meet each other on social media all the time and sometimes they become friends. Seeing a picture of an interesting bug and chatting about it is perfectly reasonable."

Suddenly a loud ringing sound interrupts the tender moment and we all twitch with varying degrees of force. Bakari grabs her phone from her back pocket and points to the screen.

"It's my mom, I have to take this." She accepts the call and the rest of us try to be as quiet as humanly and mantisly possible.

"Hi, Mom—yes, I'm okay. Yes, *really*. No, nothing broken, I was just feeling—I'm fine now. I just got a little lightheaded—no, Auntie isn't here, she had to— But it could have happened whether she was here or not—but—okay, okay! Where are you and Dad? It sounds like you're in the car, and I thought you'd be gone until tomorrow. Oh, you'll be here soon? Okay then, we'll talk more when you get home."

Bakari ends the call and looks wildly at us. "They cut their trip short after I called them from the hospital! Their connecting flight landed at the local airport an hour ago. They'll probably be here in like twenty minutes!"

Elena and I don't need to be told twice that it's definitely time to go. Bakari doesn't look happy at this abrupt leave-taking, but it can't be helped. Elena holds out a hand to Harry and he steps aboard. She gets him settled on her shoulder and gathers up her purse, then turns back to Bakari. "Everything will be okay, sweetheart. I know it will

be hard, but please remember not to talk about Harry, and not Tristan and me just yet. We'll let ourselves out."

The girl nods sadly, waves her fingers in goodbye as we leave the kitchen, then starts clearing up the dishes from our coffee break.

We hurriedly walk back through the hallway to the foyer and stop beside the trunk where Harry's aquarium is sitting. I'm feeling a little tense—okay, more than a little, and also stressed. Maybe a little whiny as well.

"Why do I feel like we're running from a crime scene and I should go start the getaway car?"

Elena gives me a tight smile as she places Harry in the aquarium. "Well, I expect it's because that's pretty much the situation we're in. Except I'm going to go start the car and you're going to carry Harry out. You should put him on the floor in back of my seat."

I automatically go into "Yes ma'am" territory and do as I'm told, but I do have to wonder when it was exactly that Elena became the boss of me. I just hope she doesn't try to drive like a getaway driver. She seems pretty calm at the moment, but that calmness actually scares me a little after what I've seen of her the past twenty-four hours. So that's me right now, scared and whiny, but I mentally ditch my inner three-year old and carry on.

I see some sort of long, silky scarf lying on the back seat, so I take that and tuck it around Harry as an added safety measure. I don't want him ping-ponging around in his aquarium if we do end up in a car chase. As I wrap him up, I distractedly wonder how to make a little seatbelt for him, but that project is obviously for another time when we're not on the run. We're all finally buckled in and secured. Harry's aquarium is snugged in behind Elena's seat and won't slide around. Elena checks the side mirror, signals, and pulls out into the street, nice and easy. As I turn to face forward I catch a glimpse of a turn signal blinking a couple of blocks behind us, and see a newish sedan pull into the driveway of the house we just left. So yeah, close call.

When Harry had become an inadvertent *La Florida* colonist so long ago, he had felt he understood the other colonists' united desire to leave the comforts of their homeland. He understood their longing for the opportunity to start anew in a completely different land, to become more than they had been. He had felt the same driving desire to see and experience something, anything, that was new and different. Harry had found that adventures including "new and different" experiences had a tendency to be not only dangerous and exciting, but also not necessarily conducive to continued life. He sadly remembered Catt's demise, a mere few weeks after they washed ashore, from the combined effects of the shipwreck and her age. She had joked at the end of having spent her last life on him, but he had felt her surprising fondness for him. He had missed her greatly.

At first, Harry had sympathized with the colonists' severe struggle to establish any comfort at all in the extremely alien tropical environment. For many years, he had watched the colonists build, plant, suffer, and die until, gradually, a foothold was gained. The humans stopped dying so quickly, their deaths came in lesser numbers, and a foreign sort of normalcy was established. With the immediate, urgent struggle for the colony's survival somewhat abated, Harry began to study the colonists rather than merely observing them at their works. He was discomfited to find that he had been incorrect about the overall driving force for the colonization. Harry came to an appalled understanding that a benign government hadn't *helped* the colonists arrive in what they came to call the New World. A tyrannical king of the old world had *sent* them to take what they could, whether it be land, gold, or power, for the benefit of the mighty kingdom. A secondary, but no less urgent, colonial impetus was the expansion of the colonists' religion to the New World. The rightful first peoples of the New World were decimated by the colonists' soldiers and diseases, then the remainder were further subjugated by the colonists' religion. Harry learned that the New World priests were not the form of pastoral, care-giving monks he remembered from his monastery life.

From the safety of his various hidden dens, during his *La Florida* tenure, Harry witnessed the settlement grow fantastically over the centuries, to become its present-day incarnation as a small, busy modern city. He had watched the railroad being built, not fully understanding at the time what it would come to mean to him. The land was eventually overrun with an incredible array of motorized vehicles, but the *train*, the train was the thing that literally moved him. He had learned a completely new, relatively easy way to travel about the countryside. Under cover of darkness, he would stealthily move from whatever little den he inhabited at the time, racing from shadow to shadow, until he reached the local railyard. After selecting the proper train and making sure he was unobserved, he would quickly climb up the exterior face of a vast iron wheel and secure himself in a dark corner of a railcar. Never a passenger car! Through trial and frustrating error, Harry had educated himself about compass points, and thereafter always made sure the train he selected was headed north. In this incremental manner he had now come to the boundary between Florida and the beginning of the territory he hoped would form his next area of adventure and discovery.

When the train he had most recently ridden halted at a small-town stop, like any experienced hobo Harry quickly jumped down to the ground and hustled to cover on the side of the tracks opposite the station platform. He watched the train pull away from the station a few minutes later, leaving the area sleepily quiet in the heat of midday. Turning away from the station, Harry peered through the thick foliage and saw that there was a lovely-looking park nearby.

There were several large live oak trees, dripping moss from their twisted branches, dotted around the park. Each live oak shaded a wooden picnic table and benches, along with the ubiquitous small barbecue welded atop a thick iron post sunk into the ground. There was also a small pond, which Harry was sure would contain the local alligator. There was always a local alligator. Despite the posted "gator here!" warning signs, the park looked like a place he could inhabit for a while. He had been traveling steadily north for some time now and was looking forward to staying in one place until the urge to wander struck him again. Before long, he had found a safe little den under the roots of the largest live oak, and thereafter lived in the park quite happily for several years. It was a calm, peaceful life in the park, "gator here!" notwithstanding.

Harry had observed the non-human Florida wildlife seemingly forever, all of which appeared to like the tropical environment just fine. During his Florida sojourn there had been an astounding variety of animals that thought they would make a good meal of him. Consequently, his ability to gather and discharge ambient energy had become a well-honed self-defense mechanism. After several life-threatening adventures Harry had decided that, like crows, snakes of all types were just no good for anyone, and they were particularly questionable for his own continued well-being. Harry's policy with snakes was zap first, then run and hide.

His interactions with the human variety of Floridian were more consistently the problem. Harry liked to think of himself as even-tempered, but he had his limits and the events of the past few hours had fully met those limits. It had to be the tropical heat. It only made sense; everyone's brain must be completely fried. Harry hadn't gone into stasis for over 450 years, so in fairness, he thought grudgingly, he could be feeling a little grouchy himself. He, too, suffered in the unrelenting heat of the Deep South; and don't get him started on the humidity. At times it seemed there wasn't sufficient oxygen in Florida for sustained breathing, let alone moving about. During the day Harry was usually able to find coolish places to hide out from the heat, so he had to admit that overall, his own situation relative to the Florida weather wasn't that bad. Except during hurricane season. Harry had developed a deep and abiding respect for hurricane season.

Harry thought these thoughts because he was currently sitting at the bottom of a clear glass jar about six inches tall, with a screwed-down lid consisting of a metal circle and another piece of flat metal that fit inside the circle. The word "Mason" was embossed on the exterior of the jar. The jar was clean, and the flat part of the lid had several holes punched in it. A few blades of grass and a stick were resting in the jar with him. At the moment, a small human girl held the jar close to her face and watched Harry with intense interest to see if he might perform any entertaining actions. He watched her right back, wondering what it was going to take to get him out of this jar. The grass was a nice touch, and he chewed on a blade of it while contemplating his immediate future, which looked questionable at best. He was not a good judge of childish age, but he thought this specimen looked particularly young. Her adults must be nearby, and Harry hoped they wouldn't feel compelled to do more than watch him eat grass.

Although sound was muffled, Harry could hear indistinct adult voices calling a name. The child jumped and quickly looked around, then stashed the jar containing Harry behind the leg of the picnic table near the tree over Harry's den. He thought this seemed to be very suspicious behavior on the part of the child, who now was sitting on a bench near the table, nonchalantly swinging its legs. Harry could glimpse the legs of approaching adults, and their voices became clearer. The deeply Southern female voice sounded exasperated and tired.

"Sarah Gail, what have we told you about runnin' off like that? Don't you know that gator could come right up out of that pond and eat you up for his dinner? I swear, Roy, I don't know how I'm supposed to get through the rest of this trip. I've had just about all I can stand of ridin' in that car."

An amused, also deeply Southern, male voice responded. "Now, Lindy, it's not that much longer till we get to the new house. A couple more hours, I'm sure y'all can make it that long. The furniture will be there tomorrow first thing and we'll all get along just fine." The voice turned more stern:

"Sarah Gail, you must stop annoyin' your mama like this. I do know that you know better. Do I have to give you a consequence?"

The small legs stopped swinging for a moment. A completely unrepentant childish voice answered. "No sir, Daddy, y'all do not need to give me a consequence. I just forgot I wasn't supposed to run off, but look, it's not that far back to the parking lot so I didn't go very far. I'm sorry, Mama, I'll tell y'all first before I run off next time."

The woman sighed and thumped something down onto the picnic table. "I think the two of you are deliberately missin' my point, and I'm too tired keep on arguin' about it. Sarah Gail, you *will not* leave my side unless I say you can." Harry heard a sulky, "Yes ma'am" from the child.

Clearly, Sarah Gail was not happy with this outcome. Harry could hear smaller thumps occurring above his glass prison, and assumed the family was settling in for a picnic. They were relatively quiet for a time, and he eavesdropped on their random comments about their trip. It seemed that Daddy had gotten a new job in the state next up from Florida; he was glad to have such a good opportunity come up so unexpectedly. Mama was excited to start looking into a new job for herself, and Sarah Gail would be starting second grade at a new school in the fall. Sarah Gail didn't sound too excited about the new school. They were moving to a new house in a small town just outside the closest urban center, and Daddy thought his commute into town wouldn't really be that bad.

Eventually, the family's picnic came to an end and they gathered up their things to head back to the car. Harry felt the beginning of panic when he saw the short legs begin to accompany the adult legs away from the park's picnic area. He was being left behind, trapped! He was pretty sure he wouldn't be able to break the glass jar, and the lid was screwed down tight. Situational analysis: pro—he'd be able to breathe, given the holes punched in the lid; con—he would likely starve, since there were only a few blades of grass left in the jar with him. He wished he'd thought of rationing sooner.

Suddenly, the short legs came running back to the table. Harry spun dizzily within the jar as the child grabbed it and shoved it into her backpack, then ran to catch up with her parents, who immediately complained about her failure to listen yet again. Daddy took the backpack from the child and quickly placed it in the car's trunk, amidst their other luggage, ignoring Sarah Gail's protests. He informed her in a no- nonsense tone that she wouldn't need her backpack for the rest of the trip, as she could very well take a nap for the next two hours and sleep off her orneriness. In response, Harry heard stamping feet and a slammed car door. Daddy sighed loudly and closed the trunk.

So began Harry's very first car ride, but he was not impressed. He felt it was an inauspicious, uncomfortable beginning for what he'd heard humans extoll as the ultimate experience. It was, however, an opportunity for him to get some much-needed rest, as there had been more than the usual excitement so far today. He arranged himself as comfortably as he could, thinking that at least he'd be safe for a while. After all, if he couldn't get out, nothing—other than humans— could get in. Harry dozed, and the trip proceeded. He woke with a jerk when the car stopped moving, momentarily confused as to his location. Then he remembered Sarah Gail. Harry had no idea what might happen next and stretched his legs to limber up for action.

Harry heard their voices as they pointed out to each other various aspects of the new house and property. Mama exhorted Sarah Gail to not run off again, and Daddy opened the car's trunk. He picked up the child's backpack and started to hand it to her, but stopped and moved it up and down, as if weighing it.

"Child, what on earth do you have in here?" Events proceeded rapidly forthwith:

Daddy unzipped the backpack, lifted out the glass jar, shook it slightly to move the grass blades around, and held it up close to his face. Harry stood up and placed his forelegs on the glass in front of him and peered out at Daddy.

Daddy gasped and involuntarily let go of the jar. Sarah Gail jumped forward to catch it, but it slipped through her small hands to smash on the concrete of the driveway. Harry was a little shaken but quickly got to his feet amidst the large pieces of broken glass.

Mama saw him and let out a very unladylike scream. Daddy lurched back and grabbed at his chest as if he felt a heart attack coming on. Sarah Gail had jumped back when the jar fell, but now reached forward as if to pick up Harry from the destruction. He worried distractedly that she might cut herself. Harry heard a swooshing sound and a fast, black shadow crossed his eyesight. He felt claws grab him, then he was airborne, dangling below the body of a large black bird. Of course, what else would it be but a crow? The bird gripped Harry with the claws of both its feet, nearly immobilizing him. Nearly, but not quite. As the crow rapidly flew away from Sarah Gail's new house, Harry wiggled, squirmed, and shifted within the cage of claws. A few minutes into his unexpected flight, Harry had managed to turn himself over. Instead of watching the ground speed past below him, now Harry shrewdly evaluated the bird's vulnerable underside. There, and there—Harry touched two of his legs to the tops of the bird's legs and released a substantial burst of energy into the crow's body.

With a loud, startled squawk, the bird lost most of its altitude and automatically opened its claws, releasing its prize. Harry fell, spreading all his legs straight out so that he floated more than crashed. He landed on something bushy, then bounced off a few lower things until he finally lay on the ground, out of breath and glad to be alive.

Harry had landed in the middle of an area planted with flowers. The planted area's owner thought of it as sort of an

English garden, but had installed a more personal, non- traditional mix of plants. The planted area extended several feet from the foundation of a house and down the front length of the house. There were no regimented rows, no organized groupings of plants. It reminded Harry of a wildflower meadow. The plants were arranged with the tallest plants in back and bushier plants in front of and around the tall flowers. Lower and thicker plants were situated toward the front, with little pockets of low-lying colors scattered at the base of the bushy plants. At ground level under the plants the air was moist and warm, and sunlight flickered through openings in the foliage overhead. Harry immediately loved this planting, despite an apparent crow infestation.

Several days passed while Harry hid out from the crows among the surrounding flowers, finding various stems and leaves that were good to eat. He had watched from beneath the blossoms as the owner groomed the plants, always either humming or singing to himself as he worked. He had a wonderful voice, and Harry loved listening to him. One day Harry heard something like a bell ringing, and saw the owner take from a back pocket a small silvery rectangle and lift it to his ear.

"Hey, this is Tristan. What's up, y'all?"

Several years later, a similar ringing sound awakened Harry from an exhausted rest in Bakari's lab.

CHAPTER FOUR

Elena pulls into the driveway at home and turns off the car. We sit there quietly for a minute, not moving, listening to the metallic pings as the engine cools down. It quickly becomes too warm without the AC on, so we slowly open the doors and exit the car. We're deathly tired, and I can't imagine how Harry might feel.

I go around to the driver's side as Elena opens the door to the back seat. She leans in and gently unwinds the scarf from around Harry. He twitches a little and seems to be asleep. I lift the aquarium out of the car, and Elena walks ahead of me to unlock the front door. Without speaking, we go into the living room and I place the aquarium on its table, making damn sure the window is locked, for whatever that's worth now. The two of us sit on the couch across from the aquarium and wordlessly observe Harry. He still hasn't moved, but I can see he's breathing regularly. Elena kicks off her shoes, and I lay my head back. Instead of feeling elated that we'd retrieved Harry, for some reason I feel numb, but I assume that's due to the aftermath of all the stress and anxiety. I turn my head to look at Elena and see that she has her eyes closed. Her face is worryingly pale.

I hear a faint rustling noise and lift my head to check on Harry. He's trying to rise but seems to be having difficulty. I immediately stand and quickly move from the couch to the aquarium. This rouses Elena and she joins me beside the aquarium. He's twitching and now I can hear tiny whimpers coming from him. If he were human, I'd say he's having a nightmare. I think he needs a cover for warmth and turn to look for around for something suitable. Suddenly Elena gasps, putting a hand to her lips in wide-eyed shock. I look at her and she wordlessly points back to Harry.

He's stopped twitching, but the energy collectors that run down his spine are glowing. We watch in stunned astonishment as the glow continues to increase, and then the separate collectors start to blink. They run in a sequence, like Christmas lights. The blinks begin to go faster and faster, until the pulsing lights become steady-state and the individual collectors appear to merge into one element, shining along Harry's back. At this point Harry opens his eyes and stands up. He tilts his head and gives us a quizzical look, then twists his head around to look at his back. He seems to be as surprised as we are.

"Wow, what is up with that?"

Elena has recovered a little, enough to talk at least, and laughs shakily. "We were kind of hoping you could tell us. Has anything like this happened before?"

Harry extends his wings and buzz-tests them. I notice that the edges of his wings look more iridescent than usual, but he seems okay to me as he flits out of the aquarium and flies around the living room a couple of times. The glowing collectors don't seem to be interfering with his movements. Elena and I warily return to our places on the couch. Harry makes a couple more circuits around the ceiling, then lands in the open area in the middle of the room.

"Hey, pal—why don't you come over here and sit with us? We can all rest for a little while and recover from this adventure. I'll make us some dinner in a few minutes."

Harry flits his wings and it looks like he's coming to us, but he stumbles and drops to his knees and we jump up in alarm. Elena immediately wants to pick him up, but I grab her hand in a tight grip. My heart is pounding and I'm inclined to move in as well, but we need to take a minute to figure out what needs to be done. There may be a process underway that we should not disrupt. We just don't know enough about Harry to know how to best help him now.

Harry gasps and stands up again, balancing on stiffened legs with his arms thrust out to the sides. The iridescent glow becomes even brighter and quickly envelops his whole body. I can't help but shout.

"Harry, tell us what to do! What is going on? Are you in pain?"

He lifts an arm toward us and vigorously shakes his head, so we unwillingly subside. I have an uneasy memory of Harry trying to explain the genesis of his being, and the inimitable universal vibrations that pertain to all living things. Is there a connection to whatever he may have done for Bakari and its effect on his own energy? I wonder if he's somehow opened a way to reach the vibrations that match him to his personal reality. I desperately try to recall what he tried to teach me.

Ambient sound suddenly becomes muffled, as if we had donned industrial-strength ear protectors. The air feels muggy and dense, almost cloying. The living room is abruptly suffused with a soft, opaque light, and the edges of everything are made diffuse, as if we inhabited an Impressionist painting.

The golden glow slowly draws across the space in front of

us, as if it's a rising fog, and overtakes visual cues until we can see only Harry in front of us. What we believed to have been reality continues to change, moment by moment. Elena and I cling to the perception of the physicality of each other. I realize that while I can feel Elena, I'm no longer physically seeing her. The two of us are taking in sensory cues that are manifestly alien to us, but our brains haven't figured out how to interpret them yet. We are bewildered and fearful, on the edge of true panic, unable to perceive clues that would inform us of our roles in this reality, or even whether we still exist as anything other than disembodied observers. We stand transfixed in astonished awe by movement in front of us: Harry seems to be shapeshifting.

The image we see of Harry is blurred, and suddenly it looks as if he shrinks, then disappears. We soundlessly shout in dismay but another image appears, that of some sort of animal with long tentacles, then another animal with paddle- like limbs, and another with four long limbs ending in pseudo-hands and feet. Each image is rapidly succeeded by another, different image, coming now so quickly that all we can perceive is a shifting shadow that changes the shape of its outline. I realize we must be seeing a progression of the body configurations Harry has experienced over time. I don't know if Harry is actually physically changing shape, or if these are somehow projections; I have no understanding of this reality. The shifting images slow, then stop, and one particular config-uration remains:

A seemingly solid individual physically stands upright before us, limned by the diffuse golden fog, well- balanced on two strong legs. It's roughly five and half feet tall, and its dark eyes give the impression of deep intelligence. The skin of its hands and feet looks tough and leathery, and except for its face, its body is covered with thick, dark hair. It has two arms, held slightly away from its sides, and its hands each have four fingers and a thumb. Its feet each have five toes. It's not wearing clothing but doesn't give the impression of nakedness. Altogether, it's very "human" looking.

We watch as this image begins to soften further around the edges. It withdraws into itself, a slow-motion implosion, then separates into two sections, one very much smaller than the other. The larger portion fades away completely. The smaller portion shrinks inwardly a bit more, then we see a sharp, clear image of Harry as I first met him. This image wavers, and then we see an image of Harry standing in front of us, back in his current configuration. We're afraid to move and can only wait for whatever might come next. I hope Harry as we know him now comes back to us again.

Harry had been resting comfortably in his aquarium when he felt a twinge in his back that grabbed his attention. He stood sharply upright and held himself motionless for a moment. The twinge continued, strengthening into a rapid series of spasms that were accompanied by sharp prickles, what a human might describe as "pins and needles." The spasms started at the base of his spine and rapidly sped outward throughout his body, then repeated. Each pulsing repetition was faster than the last and reached further into Harry's nervous system, finally becoming a connected loop of energy that surged all throughout his body.

His brain pulsed with internal lightning-like surges that matched the beat of his miniscule heart. He fell to his knees, grounding his body as his attention turned inward and focused on a single, glowing point of iridescence in the center of his perception. Harry closed his eyes to his current physical state and watched as his reality came into focus. He was vaguely aware of the presence of Tristan and Elena, but found he was unable to interact with them. He could feel their fear and love for him, but it couldn't break through whatever was happening to him how. Then, all awareness of them and his life with them vanished.

He stood alone on an utterly flat plane that extended out in all directions to ultimately vanish at an unknowable distance. There was no horizon, no delineation of knowable boundaries. The surface of the plane was suffused with a soft glow that twisted and drifted below Harry like a thin, golden ground fog, seeming to rise but not encompassing him. The ambient air was unmoving, neither warm nor chilly, and he could feel no physical connection of a body to this space and time. He had become unanchored from the Tristan-Elena reality and reformed in this one, but he did not feel fear. Harry was the disconnected Observer again.

Harry observed the Tristan-Elena reality from a distance, as if through a telescopic lens, and saw the mantis configuration transform, again and again. The transformations reached back through the eons and epochs of geologic history, showing each iteration of the physical configuration that had come into existence in Harry's reality. There were hundreds of thousands of them, and he recognized and knew them all. Harry felt a sound and tasted harmony on a non-existent breeze. His telescopic vision shrank to a pinpoint that encompassed all of time and space. He was pure energy, absolutely in tune with the universal vibrations of his true origination point. He became compressed into a beam, a wave, a laser of light that sped away from the fog-enshrouded plane, flowing through an imaginary tunnel that ended at that visionary pinpoint. He stopped.

We blink eyes that can physically see now, and our known reality resurfaces. I can feel Elena's hand in mine, see her look of astounded awe that I am absolutely sure matches mine.

Harry stands facing us and holds his arms straight out in front of him, flexing very human-looking fingers on very human-looking hands. The glowing fog is gone as suddenly as it had appeared, but there remains a barely discernable glow rising from Harry's body. The living room begins to come back into focus, and it looks unnervingly normal. Harry, on the other hand, seems to crackle with something like static electricity, which is decidedly not normal. He is no longer in a mantis configuration and now appears in an apparently genderless, unblothed, adult human form, glow notwithstanding. His form looks kind of opaque and has glittering motes visibly moving under what seems to be his skin. I have to try twice before I can speak.

"Harry, is still that you? How??"

A look of wondering joy is on his face. He lifts his hands to show us that they are, at last, shaped like human hands, complete with thumbs. He looks at us with love and laughs in delight.

"It appears I somehow broke through my own veil and can touch universal energy again. Talk about getting recharged! Hey, watch this! I can form that energy into any shape I choose."

Harry's form solidifies in front of us and he now appears indistinguishable from a human being, with no glow or glittering motes in sight. He's even generated clothing for himself. Maybe he is a superhero after all.

Harry internally inspected the infinity of glittering motes now held invisibly within his fully human form. He knew that each mote connected to another, separate reality, and that some of those realities could be physically accessed with the appropriate technologies. He closed his right hand into a tight fist and grimaced.

"I remember *everything*."

MUSICAL NOTES

₁*Magic Carpet Ride*, Steppenwolf
₂*Born to be Wild*, Steppenwolf
₃*Immigrant Song*, Led Zepplin
₄*Smoke on the Water*, Deep Purple
₅*In the End*, Black Veil Brides

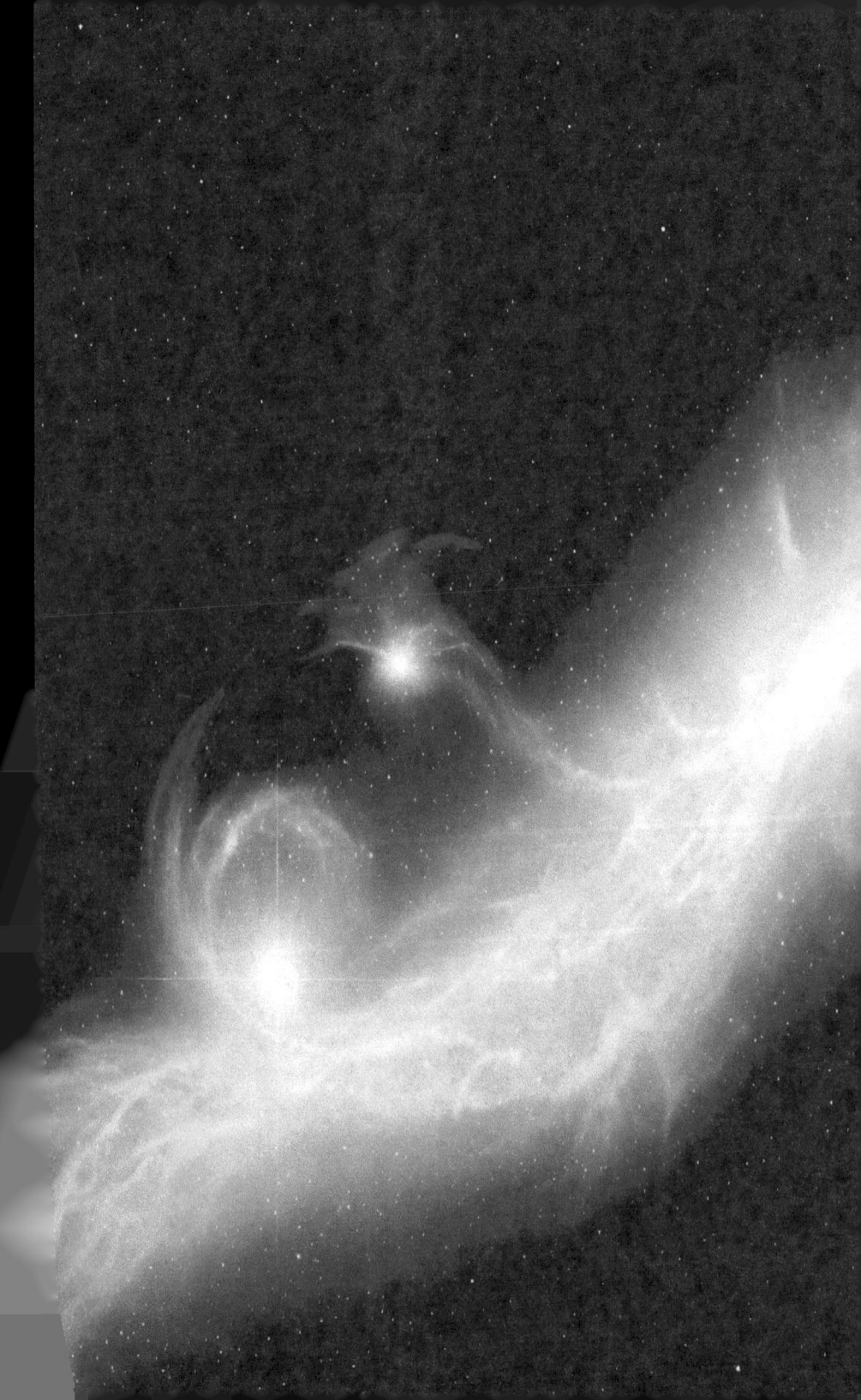

NOTE FROM THE AUTHOR

Hello, fellow traveler—

Thanks for coming along for the ride with Harry. I hope you laughed, gasped, and maybe questioned the nature of existence (or at least your Wi-Fi connection). Writing this story was a wild leap into the unknown—equal parts wonder and what-was-I-thinking—and I'm grateful you took the jump with me.

If you enjoyed the trip, I'd love for you to share your thoughts with other explorers! Even a short review helps more readers discover Harry's next misadventure:

🚀 Amazon
🌍 Goodreads
⭐ BookBub

Want to keep up with Harry's ongoing cosmic chaos? Find me on Facebook at *RealityCheck* or visit deborahdugan.com for updates, sneak peeks, and the occasional existential crisis disguised as humor.

Until next time—

Deborah Dugan

(Don't forget your towel.)

ABOUT THE AUTHOR

Deborah Dugan never outgrew her childhood obsession with the stars—she just learned to turn it into fiction. Her first stories appeared around age ten, when she decided alien civilizations probably spoke in strings of all vowels or all consonants. When that proved unpronounceable (and mildly disastrous), she pivoted to English and hasn't looked back.

A lifelong explorer of quantum physics, metaphysics, and all things extraterrestrial, Deborah's curiosity eventually evolved into *The Traveler* series—stories that blend science, humor, and the wonderfully unpredictable nature of being human.

Born in the Midwest and now based in the Pacific Northwest, she spends her time pondering the multiverse, researching new theories that make her head spin, and occasionally wondering if her coffee maker might be sentient.

Find her at deborahdugan.com or on Facebook at *Reality-Check*—preferably before the next temporal anomaly hits.

ALSO BY DEBORAH DUGAN